Other Avon Camelot Books by
Dan Gutman

BABE & ME
HONUS & ME

Coming Soon

JOHNNY HANGTIME

JACKIE
& Me

A Baseball Card Adventure

DAN GUTMAN

AN AVON CAMELOT BOOK

AVON BOOKS, INC.
1350 Avenue of the Americas
New York, New York 10019

Copyright © 1999 by Dan Gutman
Published by arrangement with the author
Library of Congress Catalog Card Number: 98-53347
ISBN: 0-380-80084-5
www.avonbooks.com

First Avon Camelot Paperback Printing: February 2000
First Avon Camelot Hardcover Printing: March 1999

CAMELOT TRADEMARK REG. U.S. PAT. OFF. AND IN OTHER COUNTRIES, MARCA REGISTRADA, HECHO EN U.S.A.

Printed in the U.S.A.

OPM 10 9 8 7 6 5 4 3 2

For Stephanie Siegel

*"A life is not important
except in the impact it has on other lives."*

—JACKIE ROBINSON'S EPITAPH

INTRODUCTION

THERE'S SOMETHING YOU SHOULD KNOW ABOUT ME. I'VE got a special power.

It's sort of like a sixth sense. Nobody knows about it except my mom and dad. I discovered it when I was very little. My dad had given me a bunch of baseball cards. As I was handling the cards, I felt a funny tingling sensation in my fingertips. Buzzy. It sort of felt like the feeling you get when you touch a TV screen with the power on.

I didn't think too much about the tingling sensation when I was a little kid. I just figured all kids had the same feeling when they held a baseball card in their hands.

But then I discovered what that tingling sensation meant. One day, I went to sleep with a very old baseball card in my hand. When I woke up, I was in the year 1909.

I know it sounds crazy. You may not believe me.

That's okay. You don't have to believe me. I know what happened. I could use baseball cards to travel through time. For me, a baseball card was like a time machine. The tingling sensation was the signal that I was about to go on a trip, back to the year of the baseball card in my hand.

The first time this happened, it was a pretty exciting—and frightening—experience. When I got back from my "trip," I didn't think I would ever take another one.

But when you've got a special power—this gift—it seems a shame not to use it. So I did. This is the story of what happened.

Joe Stoshack

1

THE BRAWL

"YOU CAN'T HIT, STOSHACK!" BOBBY FULLER YELLED AT ME from the pitcher's mound. "You couldn't hit water if you fell off a boat!"

I stepped into the batter's box. Bobby Fuller busted my chops all last season. Now it was our first practice game and he was starting in again. I dug my left toe into the dirt and got set for his first pitch.

"You're ugly, too, Stoshack."

Fuller knows he can rattle me. That's why he does it. My team, the Yellow Jackets, had a one-run lead in the fifth inning. The runners at second and third took their leads. Two outs. A hit would put the game out of reach. Fuller needed to strike me out. I was doing my best not to let him get to me.

"Did I mention stupid?" Fuller asked. I pumped my bat back and forth. "You're stupid, too, Stoshack."

A few of Fuller's teammates snickered. I felt the blood rushing to my face. *Try to act like it doesn't bother you*, I said to myself. *Try to act like it doesn't bother you.*

"You gonna take that, Stoshack?" the catcher whispered to me, quietly enough so that even the umpire wouldn't hear. "What kind of a wimp are you?"

It would be so *easy*. I could just turn around, take my bat, and brain the catcher with it. Do some real damage. His mask would provide only so much protection. That would shut him up. And it would feel *so* good.

"Stick it in his ear, Bobby!" the shortstop hollered.

The coaches are always telling us about the importance of sportsmanship. The Louisville Little League has strict rules about how we're supposed to act, and what we're allowed to say to the other team during our games. I guess Bobby Fuller and his teammates never got the message. Their coach didn't seem to care.

"You know you can't hit me, Stoshack," Fuller said as he looked in for the sign. "Because you're a big, slow, ugly, dumb *Polack*!"

That's it.

Call me ugly. Call me stupid. Say I can't hit. But don't make fun of my nationality or you're gonna pay.

I didn't wait for the pitch. I brought the bat back and flung it at Fuller as hard as I could. It went spinning out of my hands and flew toward the pitcher's mound, about thigh high. Fuller freaked. He jumped to avoid the bat shooting toward him. It zipped about an inch below his heels and skittered all the way to second base.

"This ain't hockey, Stoshack," the umpire warned me. "You're out of the game!"

I didn't care. When I saw Fuller skip out of the way of my bat, I lost control. I made a fist and charged the mound. I was ready to rip his head off. Fuller flung away his glove and put his fists up.

"You wanna fight, Stoshack?" he laughed. "I'll kick your butt!"

I could see Fuller's teammates converging on the mound to defend him, but it didn't matter. There could have been a hundred guys out there. I still would have tried to bust Fuller's skull in.

Before I reached the mound, the catcher jumped on my back from behind and knocked me down. By that time, my teammates had rushed off the bench and stormed the field.

I couldn't tell exactly what happened next. I was at the bottom of a pile of bodies. There was a lot of yelling. I felt some punches being thrown at my head. Somebody stepped on my hand. Mostly, it was just the weight of a bunch of kids on top of me.

It took about ten minutes for the coaches to calm everybody down and peel all the kids off the pile. I was the last one to get up. I was okay, but my hand was throbbing. Coach Hutchinson wrapped his burly arm around my shoulder and steered me roughly back to the bench.

"The season hasn't even started yet!" he complained. "What are you trying to do, get yourself suspended?"

I glanced at Fuller. Nobody laid a glove on him. He

smirked and turned away. I tore away from Coach Hutchinson and went after Fuller again.

"I'm gonna kill you, Fuller!" I yelled.

This time the umpire tackled me, sending me face-first into the dirt around home plate. He lay on top of me, not letting me move.

"You got a problem, young man," the ump said in my ear. "You're not gonna play in this league again until you solve it."

Coach Hutchinson was furious with me. So was my mom. The Yellow Jackets forfeited the game. My left pinky was sprained. I was suspended from the Little League indefinitely.

2

THE TINGLING SENSATION

AFTER IT WAS ALL OVER, I REALIZED HOW STUPID I HAD BEEN to start the fight with Fuller. He did it all on purpose, I realized. He was probably afraid I was going to get a hit and drive in both runs. He knew that if I started a fight with him, the game would be forfeited and his team would win.

He was right about one thing. I *am* dumb. Sometimes I just can't control my anger.

"I lost it, Mom," I said as my mother held an ice-pack against my hand. "I'm sorry."

My mom is a nurse at University of Louisville Hospital. She made a splint for my finger and gave me a speech about controlling my temper.

I didn't want to face the kids at school the next day after making such a fool of myself. I brought up the idea of staying home, but Mom shot it down.

"Nice try, Joey," she said. "But you're going to have to do a lot better than a sprained pinky."

* 　 * 　 *

Louisville is in Kentucky, about seventy-five miles west of Lexington, on the Ohio River. The Louisville Slugger bat was invented here. Kentucky Fried Chicken started in nearby Corbin.

Kentucky fought on the side of the South during the Civil War. There was slavery here. It was a terrible thing, of course. I guess the white people back then didn't realize how wrong it was, or decided to *ignore* how wrong it was. It's hard to understand today how they could think and act that way back then, but I guess it was just a different time and people had different attitudes.

These days, my class at school is a mixture of white kids and black kids and we get along pretty well. I'm white and most of the kids I know are white, but it's not out of prejudice or anything. I don't think it is, anyway. The black kids make friends mostly with other black kids and they hang together. That's just the way it is.

I'm bringing all this up because February is Black History Month, and most of my teachers were making it part of our studies. Mrs. Levitt, my history teacher, shushed us when we sat down for class on Monday morning.

"Who wants to win a prize?" she asked.

"Oooh! Oooh!" we all moaned, waving our hands around to attract her attention.

"You're going to have to give an oral report," she added.

Everybody groaned and put their hands down.

"I want each of you to choose a famous African-

American," she said as she walked around the room, passing out a sheet of paper with names on it. "I want you to research that person's life and do a report on him or her. You'll have plenty of time. The reports won't be due until May. And there will be a prize for the best report."

"What's the prize?" somebody asked.

"Four tickets to Kentucky Kingdom," said Mrs. Levitt.

"Oooh!" everybody moaned. Kentucky Kingdom is this really cool amusement park with seventy-five rides. One of them is a sixteen-story free-fall. Kentucky Kingdom costs something like twenty-five dollars to get in, and I've never been there.

"Does it matter if the person is dead or alive?" somebody asked. A few of the kids in the back of the room laughed.

"No," Mrs. Levitt replied. "But I don't want you to write about a player on your favorite sports team."

She glanced at me. She knows I'm a sports nut, and I'm always trying to get away with sneaking sports into my schoolwork instead of the stuff we need to learn. Like, in math, I convinced Mrs. Levitt to use batting averages to help us learn multiplication and division. In music, I always ask if we can sing sports songs. In art, I'm always drawing pictures of athletes.

"I want you to write about men and women who made a real contribution to American society."

"How about *dead* athletes?" I asked, and a few kids giggled.

"Well . . ." Mrs. Levitt said, thinking it over. "As

long as you select an athlete who contributed something to the world."

"What if they're retired but not quite dead yet?"
I asked.

"Joe," she said sternly, "you know the assignment."

I scanned the list that she had handed out—*Freder-
ick Douglass . . . Marian Anderson . . . Langston
Hughes . . .*

Howie Wohl, the kid behind me, slipped me a note.
DID LANGSTON HUGHES PLAY FOR THE
LAKERS?

I scribbled HE WAS A POET, EINSTEIN! and
passed the note back to him. Then I continued going
down the list—*Benjamin Banneker . . . W.E.B. Du
Bois . . . Paul Robeson . . . Sojourner Truth . . . Booker
T. Washington . . . Jackie Robinson . . .*

Jackie Robinson! The baseball player! *I could go
back in time and meet Jackie Robinson*, I thought.

I didn't know much about Robinson. I remember
reading on the back of some baseball card that African-American players were banned from the major
leagues for about sixty years. Robinson was the first
player to break the "color barrier." He played for the
Brooklyn Dodgers before they moved to California
and became the Los Angeles Dodgers—my favorite
team. That was all I knew about him.

But if I were to go back in time and actually *meet*
the guy, I could find out all I needed to know. I would
see, with my own eyes, what it was like for him to
break the color barrier. I was a cinch to get the best
mark on the report and win the trip to Kentucky
Kingdom.

I was psyched. After school I rushed home and grabbed *The Baseball Encyclopedia* to see what year Jackie Robinson broke into the big leagues.

Nineteen forty-seven. Now all I needed to do was get a 1947 Jackie Robinson baseball card.

3

A GREAT DEAL

ABOUT A MILE FROM MY HOUSE, IN A STRIP MALL OFF Shelbyville Road on the east side of Louisville, is a baseball card store called Flip's Fan Club. The owner, Flip Valentini, sells new cards, old cards, comic books, and all kinds of collectibles from Mickey Mouse to Marilyn Monroe. He also buys all kinds of stuff, and has some valuable things in his collection.

Flip is a cool guy because he's really old—sixty or seventy or something—but he still reads comic books and cares about stuff that usually only kids care about. He told me he got the nickname Flip because when he was a kid, he and his friends played a game where they would flip baseball cards against a wall. The kid whose card landed closest to the wall got to keep all the cards that were flipped.

It's hard to believe that kids actually used to do that. I mean, today those cards would be worth a

About a mile from my house, in a strip mall on the east side of Louisville, is a baseball card store called Flip's Fan Club.

fortune. If Flip had taken care of his cards when he was a kid, he'd be rich today.

"How was I to know that baseball cards would be worth anything?" Flip laughs.

He told me that when he grew up and left home, his mother threw his entire baseball card collection in the garbage. Can you imagine? Hundreds of cards from the 1940s and 1950s trashed?

It must have traumatized him for life, I figure. That's probably why Flip started a business buying and selling cards when he retired. Flip's Fan Club opened about six months ago. The card store I used to go to—Home Run Heaven—went out of business and Flip bought up all the stock.

I ride my bike over to Flip's Fan Club all the time, so Flip knows me and is pretty nice to me. I took off my bike helmet and replaced it with my Dodgers cap before I entered the store.

"Long time no see, Joey!" he greeted me. There were only a few other people in the store. "What can I doferya today?"

"I'm looking for a Jackie Robinson card, Mr. Valentini."

"Brooklyn Dodgers," Flip mumbled, reaching under the counter. "Dem Bums. My team. I grew up in Brooklyn, y'know. Lemme see . . . I got a '51 Robinson."

"I need a 1947," I replied. "His rookie year."

"There are no 1947 cards, Joey."

"What?!"

"They didn't print 'em. During World War II, the government needed as much paper and ink as they could get. The baseball card companies had to stop production. They didn't crank up again until 1948. There *was* no 1947 Jackie Robinson rookie card, Joey."

My heart sank. I wouldn't be able to make my trip back in time after all. Flip saw how disappointed I was.

"I *do* have something," he said. "But I gotta warn ya that it's pretty expensive."

He went to the back of the store and returned a few minutes later with a batch of cards in his hand.

"In 1947, Jackie Robinson was signed by the Bond Bread company to endorse their products," Flip said. "Bond issued a set of thirteen cards, with Robinson caught in a different pose for each one. They're very rare. A guy sold me the complete set a while ago."

"How much is it worth?" I asked.

"More than you have in your pocket, I bet."

"How much?"

"Five . . . thousand dollars."

I exhaled.

"Joey, I'll give it to you for forty-five hundred because you're a regular customer."

Forty-five hundred dollars! I had a twenty-dollar bill in my pocket. I had been hoping I would be able to use it to get a Robinson card, and maybe a little change back. To come up with that amount, I would have to mow about five hundred lawns. And I didn't even have a power mower.

"How much is just *one* card?"

"I hate to break up the set," Flip said, "because it

makes it hard to sell the rest of it. But for you? One card? Four hundred dollars."

Flip handed me one of the cards. There was a black-and-white photo of Jackie Robinson on the front. He was sliding into home plate. The umpire had thrown his arms out to the sides to indicate Robinson was safe.

On the back of the card was a picture of a loaf of bread. Above the bread was Robinson's signature after the words, HOMOGENIZED BOND MAKES A HIT WITH ME EVERY TIME. Below the bread were the words, FOLKS, WHY NOT EAT THE BREAD THAT JACKIE EATS? HOMOGENIZED BOND!

Right away I could feel that tingling sensation in my fingertips. That's how I could tell I would be able to use the card to travel back through time. Four hundred dollars was still way out of my league. But I had an idea.

"If I could come up with four hundred," I asked Flip, "could I buy the card from you, and then sell it back to you for four hundred? I only need the card for a few days."

"Whydya need a '47 Robinson card so badly?" Flip asked, looking at me a little suspiciously. "And whydya only need it fera few days?"

"I'm a Dodger fan," I said, tipping my cap, "and it's kind of a secret."

Flip looked me over, as if he were trying to decide if he could trust me or not.

"I shouldn't be doin' dis," he finally said, putting the card in a plastic holder. "But I'm a lousy businessman and you love the Bums. Take the card. No charge. Bring it back in a few days and we'll call it square. Does that sound like a deal to you?"

"Yeah!"

"Now get outta here before I change my mind. And take good care of that card, y'hear?" Flip warned, pointing his stubby finger at me. "If you lose it or damage it, I'm gonna havta charge you for it."

We shook hands. I put the card in my backpack and pedaled home with my treasure.

4

GOING BACK, BACK, BACK . . .

MOM WAS NOT *ENTIRELY* SUPPORTIVE WHEN I TOLD HER OF my plan to go back to 1947 to meet Jackie Robinson.

"N-O," she spelled. "No more time travel. Out of the question."

"But, Mom!"

"What if somebody ticks you off and you lose your temper in the past?" she asked. "You could get into a lot of trouble."

"I won't lose my temper," I promised.

"What if you get hurt? The doctors in 1947 didn't know what we know today. They didn't have our medicines, CAT scans . . ."

"I'm not gonna get hurt!" I assured her.

"What about school?"

"I won't miss any school. Last time I went back in time, it was the next morning here when I came back. And I'm gonna do a report on it, Mom! For history class. It's gonna be *educational*."

Mom's a sucker for anything educational. I could ride my bike off a cliff, and if I could convince her that I did it so I would learn about the physics of falling objects, she would probably say it was all right. But this time she wouldn't bite.

"Joey, I said no."

"You can't stop me, y'know," I announced angrily. "I could just go and you would never even know I was gone."

"Joe, when I wake up in the morning, I expect you to be in your bed. Every day. That's all I have to say."

"I will be, Mom. I promise."

Mom gave me one of those hugs where she won't let go for a long time.

"I know I can't stop you if you really want to do this," she said, looking me in the eye. "If you go against my wishes, just do me one favor—be careful. And please bring along a coat."

"Baseball season begins in April, Mom. It's springtime."

"What about global warming?" she pointed out. "They say the earth is a lot warmer than it used to be. There's a hole in the ozone layer now."

I rolled my eyes and she caught me.

"I just worry about you, Joey," Mom said, mussing up my hair. "You've never been to New York City. It's *dangerous*. What if you run into Al Capone or some other criminal?"

"I'm just going to meet Jackie Robinson, Mom. Then I'll come right home. Besides, people always say how much safer New York City used to be a long time ago. Isn't that why the past is called the good old days?"

A few nights later, after dinner, the doorbell rang. Mom motioned for me to get it, so I knew it had to be my dad. My parents have been divorced for a couple of years now. They're on speaking terms, but Mom prefers not to speak with Dad if she doesn't have to. Dad lives in Louisville too, and we get together once a week or so.

Mom scurried off to the kitchen. I let Dad inside. He was carrying a suitcase. I noticed that my initials—J.S.—were embroidered on it.

"Hey buddy," he said, overly enthusiastic. "Mom told me you got the itch to travel through time again!"

"Yeah, I think I'm ready to try another trip, Dad."

"In that case, I brought you something."

He reached into his jacket pocket, pulled out a baseball card, and handed it to me. I recognized the face of Babe Ruth right away. I flipped the card over and looked at the back. It was from the 1930s, and probably worth a hundred bucks or more.

Dad's a machinist at a Louisville factory. He doesn't make a lot of money, not enough to be throwing around presents like this one.

"Wow!" I exclaimed.

"I want you to have it," he said. "You can use it, you know."

I knew exactly what he meant. Dad grew up in New York and he's always been a huge Yankees fan. His favorite player of all time was Babe Ruth.

When Dad was a kid, he told me, he and his friends

would wait outside Yankee Stadium after games for the players to leave the clubhouse. Then they would ambush the players for autographs before they were able to get to their cars. Dad built up his autograph collection over the years and now he's got just about all the Yankee greats, except for Ruth. Babe Ruth died before my dad was even born, and his autograph is very expensive.

Ever since we discovered I could travel through time using baseball cards, Dad had been hinting around that I should pay a visit to Babe Ruth and get his autograph. That's why he got me the Ruth card.

"Did I ever tell you the story of Ruth's called shot?" Dad asked.

Only a million times. In the fifth inning of game three of the 1932 World Series, the Babe hit a monstrous home run over the center-field fence at Wrigley Field in Chicago. According to baseball legend, just before the pitch Ruth pointed toward center field and said he was going to sock the ball there.

Some people say Ruth called his shot. Others say he never even pointed at the fence at all. There's a film that was taken of that at-bat, but it's too fuzzy to tell exactly what's going on. Dad wanted me to go back to 1932 and find out if Babe Ruth really called his shot or not.

"It's the biggest mystery in all of sports, Joe," he said excitedly. "And you're the only person in the world who can solve it."

"Dad, I really want to meet Jackie Robinson," I said. "Maybe I'll visit Babe Ruth another time."

Dad sighed. He knew I'm pretty stubborn and he wasn't going to talk me into it.

"What's in the suitcase?" I asked.

"Nothing," he said, handing it to me. "It's empty."

"Dad, I already have a suitcase."

"It's not for your clothes," he whispered, like he didn't want Mom to hear.

I knew my dad pretty well. I had a feeling about what he had in mind.

"Joey, when you go back in time, I want you to buy up as many baseball cards as you can," he said, taking out his wallet and peeling off a ten-dollar bill. "Fill the suitcase with them. Then bring the cards back with you. Can you imagine how much a suitcase full of mint condition cards from the 1940s will be worth in today's market? Thousands."

I looked at him. My aim in going to 1947 wasn't to make money. I just wanted to meet Jackie Robinson. What he was asking me to do probably wasn't illegal. But something about it didn't feel right. And besides, I told him, baseball cards weren't even *printed* in 1947.

"If Bond Bread made a set of Robinson cards," Dad insisted, "I'm sure other companies printed baseball cards too. People had cards from before the war. They'll probably give them to you for nothing."

My dad is my dad. I took the ten-dollar bill and stuffed it in my pocket.

I filled a duffel bag with T-shirts and blue jeans, clothes that I hoped wouldn't attract too much notice in 1947. I also packed my toothbrush, my Game Boy—stuff I would bring with me on any long trip.

I had almost forgotten to pack the most important thing—a baseball card. Just as I needed a 1947 card to get to 1947, I would need a present-day card to get home again. Baseball cards, to me, were sort of like plane tickets. They took me to the past, and then back to the present.

I went through my card collection. It didn't really matter which current-day card I chose. Even a card of the worst benchwarmer in the big leagues would get me back home when I needed to return.

No, I decided. When I travel, I want to travel in *style*. I pulled out my best card. Junior. Ken Griffey Jr. would get me back home when I was ready to leave the past. I slipped the Griffey card in my wallet.

Mom knocked on my door. I thought she was going to try to talk me out of taking my trip one more time. She didn't. She simply handed me a Styrofoam cooler, undoubtedly packed with enough food to last a year.

"You be careful now, you hear?" she said.

I promised that I would, and she put the cooler at the end of my bed. After I put my duffel bag and dad's empty suitcase on the bed too, there wasn't a whole lot of room left for me. I squeezed on somehow and took out the Jackie Robinson card. Mom kissed me on the forehead and shut the door behind her.

I held the card with both hands against my chest and thought of the year 1947. The Brooklyn Dodgers. New York.

It wasn't long before I felt that tingling sensation in

my fingertips, and then all over my body. It was a pleasant feeling, almost like a cat purring in your ear.

Jackie Robinson! What was he like? I wondered. What must it have *been* like for him? What did he have to put up with, being the first African-American to play in the big leagues in the twentieth century? I wished I could see what he experienced.

And then I dropped off to sleep.

5

A SLIGHT CHANGE

WHEN YOU SEE TIME TRAVEL STORIES IN THE MOVIES, THE person who travels through time always seems to wind up exactly where he was planning to go. If he wanted to visit Napoleon, his time machine takes him to Napoleon's living room. If she wanted to witness the invention of fire, she just happens to "land" at the exact moment some caveperson accidently smacked two rocks together to ignite the first spark.

Uncanny, isn't it? That's the movies for you. In the real world, though, things don't always work out so perfectly.

When I lay down on my bed and prepared for my trip, I was expecting I'd wake up at Ebbets Field in Brooklyn, New York. That's where the Dodgers used to play. Or maybe I would wind up at Jackie Robinson's house. Or wherever he happened to be at the time.

But when I woke up, I realized immediately that I

wasn't at any of those places. It was totally dark and cold. I was outdoors, at night. The ground was hard. Concrete. Shards of glass were littered around. There were noises of cars honking. I was scared.

"Hello?" I whispered, hesitantly. "Anyone here?"

Somebody groaned. The voice came from about twenty feet away. Carefully, I stood up and felt around me. All the stuff I had brought along seemed to be there. I felt my way toward the voice. My eyes were beginning to adjust to the dark. I could make out the form of a man.

"Are you okay, mister?" I asked.

The guy groaned again. He was lying on his side, clutching his arm. When I got closer, I could tell he was a black man. He was bleeding pretty heavily from his left arm near the hand.

"A broken bottle," he whispered. "I tried to fight them off. . . ."

My mom told me she has seen people walk into the emergency room after getting attacked. The natural reaction is to use your hands to protect yourself. Unfortunately, that exposes your wrists, the site of a major artery leading away from the heart. If the attacker has a knife or some other sharp object, that artery can be opened pretty easily. If you lose too much blood, it's all over.

I took off my belt as quickly as I could and wrapped it around the guy's forearm. Mom told me the important thing to do when an artery is open is to block off the blood flow somewhere between the wound and the heart. I tightened the belt around the guy's arm and held it there. In a little while the bleeding seemed to have stopped and the guy was able to sit up.

"Thank you, brother," he said. "I hate to think what mighta happened if you hadn'ta come along."

"It was nothing," I said.

"Saving a man's life? I'd say that's somethin'."

"Are you Jackie Robinson?"

"No," he groaned. "Name is Bankhead. Dan Bankhead." He stuck out his right hand—his good hand—and I shook it.

"Joe Stoshack," I said.

He didn't let go of my hand, so I grabbed on tight and pulled him up to a standing position. He was about six feet tall, and athletically built.

Dan Bankhead? What the heck was I doing in a dark alley with *this* guy? I wanted to meet Jackie Robinson. Something must have gone terribly wrong. I must have messed up somehow. Maybe I didn't go back to 1947. I had no idea where I was, or when.

"If you want," Bankhead said, "I can *take* you to Jackie Robinson."

"You *know* Jackie Robinson?" I asked.

"Follow me, kid."

Bankhead picked up my duffel bag with his good hand. I grabbed the cooler and my suitcase. I didn't want anyone to touch the suitcase. People might start asking questions. Nobody walks around with an empty suitcase unless they're planning to fill it with something.

Bankhead led me out of the alley. As soon as we reached the opening, I was nearly blinded by the light. Flashing signs. Enormous billboards. There

must have been ten theaters on the street. ETHEL
MERMAN IN ANNIE GET YOUR GUN announced one of
them in flashing lights. BRIGADOON. FINIAN'S RAINBOW.
On top of one building was a giant billboard of a cup of
coffee, and real steam pouring out of it.

I had landed in New York City, I was sure of that.

In Louisville at night, most everybody's indoors.
Watching TV. Sleeping. Whatever. Here, it was like
daytime. There were people all over the place, rushing around as if they had a place to go. The men all
wore hats. Old cars filled the street. Big yellow taxis,
with checkerboard patterns running down the sides.

"You must be new in town," commented Bankhead.
"Only tourists gawk like that."

"Where are we?" I asked.

Then I noticed a street sign at the intersection. It
said 43RD STREET in one direction and BROADWAY in
the other.

"Times Square," Bankhead replied. "The center of
the universe."

"I thought New York City was supposed to be safe
in the good old days."

"The good old days?" Bankhead chuckled. "Good for
white folks, maybe. Ain't so hot for Negroes who stray
outta Harlem."

"Why did they do this to you?"

"Three guesses," Bankhead said. "And the first two
don't count."

He led me across the street and we walked down
Broadway in the direction of 42nd Street. There were
more theaters, movie theaters. Bob Hope in *My Fa-*

vorite Brunette. Abbott and Costello in *Buck Privates Come Home.* Jimmy Stewart in *It's a Wonderful Life.*

"My dad has that on tape," I remarked.

Bankhead looked at me strangely. Oops! I'd better be more careful about what I say, I realized. They didn't have VCRs in 1947. For all I knew, they didn't even have TV. I wasn't sure how people would react if they found out I came from the future.

As we walked past 40th Street and 39th Street, there were fewer lights and the neighborhood became noticeably less busy. Bankhead told me he was a baseball player, a pitcher with the Memphis Red Sox in the Negro Leagues. He had been a Marine during World War II. His twenty-seventh birthday would be coming up in two weeks.

"With a little luck, I'm gonna celebrate it by pitching for the Dodgers," he said proudly.

Fat chance. I knew perfectly well that Jackie Robinson was the only African-American on the Dodgers.

At the corner of 36th Street and Broadway there was a shoe store. The lights weren't on inside, but as we walked by I saw a black kid in the window. He looked to be about my age.

There was something strange about the kid, I noticed. I stopped and looked at him. He looked straight at me without moving. *Maybe he's robbing the store,* I thought. *Should I call a policeman?*

The kid just kept staring at me. If he was robbing the place, he wouldn't waste time looking at *me.* I waved to the kid. He waved back at me, like he knew me.

As I turned my head to the left to tell Bankhead

about the black kid in the window, I noticed the kid turned his head at the same time. I turned my head to the other side. So did the black kid.

Wait a minute! That was no window! It was a *mirror*. I was looking at my *reflection*!

I quickly brought my hand up to my face. The skin was dark.

I had turned into a black kid!

Frantically, I touched the skin on my arms. It felt like it always did, but the darkness wouldn't rub off. I looked in the mirror again and touched my hair.

I must have let out a horrified gasp, because Bankhead and a few passersby looked at me curiously.

"Joe, are you okay?" Bankhead asked. "You're white as a ghost."

If he only knew!

"Come on, Joe," Bankhead said, a certain annoyance in his voice now. "I don't have all night. Do you want to meet Jackie Robinson or not?"

What happened, it occurred to me, wasn't so crazy. The first time I traveled back through time, I had gone to bed wishing I was a grown-up. When I woke up in 1909, I *was* one. *This* time, I went to bed wishing I could experience what Jackie Robinson experienced when he was breaking into the big leagues. The only way that could happen would be if *I* became an African-American. So when I woke up in 1947, I was black.

Traveling back in time wasn't quite as simple as I had imagined.

6

THE ROBINSON FAMILY

I WAS STILL TRYING TO GET PAST THE INITIAL SHOCK OF realizing I was a black kid when Dan Bankhead stopped at 34th Street. A huge building took up the entire block there. The sign across the front read MACY'S.

I'd heard of Macy's. They have that Thanksgiving Day parade every year. It was probably the most famous store in the world. Jackie Robinson lived in *Macy's*?

Bankhead led me across Broadway to the other side of the street. He stopped in front of a much smaller building. There was a small sign on it: MCALPIN HOTEL. We walked up the steps and into the lobby.

"Mr. Robinson's room, please?" Bankhead asked the desk clerk politely. He looked at us disgustedly. Bankhead still had some blood on him, and he was pretty messed up. But the desk clerk told him the room number anyway and we walked upstairs.

Bankhead stopped in front of the door and did his best to straighten himself up, brushing his clothes in a futile effort to smooth out the wrinkles. Then he knocked on the door.

"Who *is* it?" a woman's voice hollered from inside.

"Danny," Bankhead replied, winking at me, "and a friend."

The door cracked open and I could see the face of a black lady. She struggled to get the door open without dropping the tiny baby in her arms. The lady appeared to be in her early twenties.

"Danny, what *happened* to you?" she asked, alarmed. "And who's your young friend?"

"I'll be fine, Rachel. This fine young man wants to meet Jackie."

The bedroom door opened, and out strolled a man with a pigeon-toed walk I had seen only in photos. For the moment, I wasn't thinking about the color of my skin. Here I was, meeting the great Jackie Robinson. The Jackie Robinson who was not only a member of the Baseball Hall of Fame, but also one of the most famous and important Americans of the twentieth century.

Goose pimples rose on my arms. I could hardly wait to get back home and start writing my report.

"Danny, who did this to you?" Jackie asked, ignoring me for the moment.

His voice was a shock. He was a big, strong man, but he had a high-pitched voice like a boy.

"I didn't catch their names," Bankhead replied.

The old photos of Jackie Robinson don't do him justice. He was a very handsome man. His skin was dark, so dark it was almost black. He was wearing gray slacks and a white shirt, which made his skin seem even darker. He was a little shorter than Dan Bankhead, but more muscular. His eyes were deep, intense. He turned toward me and stared right at me. He gripped me with his eyes.

"Who's the kid?" Jackie asked.

"Joe Stoshack," I volunteered, grabbing for his hand. "Everybody calls me Stosh. It's a pleasure and honor to meet you, Mr. Robinson."

"Everybody calls me Jack, Stosh."

Mrs. Robinson handed the baby over to Jackie while she took Bankhead to the kitchen to tend to his wounds. The baby didn't like being jostled and let out a yelp.

"Shhh," Jackie cooed, "it's way past your bedtime, sugar lump."

I couldn't tell if the baby was a boy or a girl. I didn't want to say the wrong thing and offend anybody.

"What's the baby's name?" I asked, playing it safe.

"Jackie," Jackie replied.

Big help! Jackie could be a boy's name *or* a girl's name.

"He's nineteen weeks old," Jackie said, glancing at the bags I had brought with me. "Where's your mama, son?"

I wasn't sure what to say. I was hesitant to tell anyone the whole story of how I traveled back through time. It was too unbelievable. They might think I was putting them on. Or that I was crazy.

"Where's your mama, Stosh?" Jackie repeated.

"Home."

"Where's home?"

"Louisville, Kentucky."

"My word! Are you a runaway?"

"No."

"In some kind of trouble?"

"No."

"Did your mama send you here?"

"Not exactly."

"Son, I don't have time for guessing games," Jackie snapped. His steely eyes flashed from warmth to anger in an instant. I could see he had a quick temper, like me. I made a mental note to try not to make him angry again.

Mrs. Robinson came back out of the kitchen with Dan Bankhead. I guessed that she must be a nurse, like my mom. Bankhead was all cleaned up and fresh bandages had been expertly applied to his wounds.

"Jack," Mrs. Robinson said, "Danny says this boy may have saved his life."

That softened Jackie a bit. He thanked me with his eyes. Bankhead said he had to go, and Jackie led him to the door. Bankhead thanked me again for helping him and said goodnight. Then Jackie cooed to Jackie Jr. that it was time to go back to sleep as he carried him into the bedroom.

"Your mama packed enough food for an army," Mrs. Robinson said, putting my cooler on the counter. "Where were you planning to sleep tonight?"

"I hadn't really thought about it, ma'am."

"A young boy like you just shows up at somebody's house at night with a suitcase, and you have no idea where you're going to sleep?"

"It—it's a long story, ma'am," I stuttered, backing toward the door. "Maybe I'd better be leaving."

"Don't be crazy," she replied. "You can sleep on the couch. Tomorrow we'll try to find your mama."

"Thank you, ma'am."

"It's the least we can do after what you did for Danny," Jackie called out from the other room. "Our house is your house."

While Mrs. Robinson put sheets and covers on the couch in the living room, I looked around the place. It was tiny, certainly not a place I would expect a big star like Jackie Robinson to live. The couch took up a big part of the living room. There was no TV set. Bottles and diapers and baby toys were scattered around.

Time travel is exhausting. As soon as Mrs. Robinson finished making the couch up for me, I dove into it.

"What's today's date?" I asked before she turned off the light.

"Monday, April 14th."

"Nineteen forty-seven?"

"Of *course* 1947," she replied, looking at me curiously. Then she flipped off the light.

I couldn't sleep. Can you blame me? Here I was, more than fifty years into the past, sleeping on Jackie Robinson's couch, and I had somehow been turned into a black kid! I was too nervous and scared to sleep.

It would have been impossible to sleep anyway, because Jackie Jr. kept waking up and crying every few hours during the night. The first time, Mrs. Robinson tiptoed out to the kitchen to warm up a bottle and feed it to the baby. The next time, Jackie did the honors.

Sometime in the middle of the night, after he fed the baby, I saw Jackie tiptoe back into the kitchen. He poured himself a glass of milk, then spooned some sugar into it and stirred it up. Then he took a bag of bread out of the refrigerator and took out a slice. He sat down, dunked the bread in the milk, and bit off a piece.

"Can't sleep, huh?" I whispered.

Jackie jumped out of his chair, almost spilling the milk all over himself. He must have forgotten I was sleeping on the couch.

"Opening day jitters," Jackie said, sponging milk off the table.

"Baseball season starts tomorrow?"

"Yeah."

"I hope you get some hits."

"It's not just about hits, Stosh," he said softly, looking at me with those eyes.

"What's it about, then?" I asked.

Jackie took a long time before answering.

"My grandfather was a slave in Georgia. My father was a sharecropper. All their lives, they never had a chance to better themselves. They were never *allowed* to better themselves because they were Negroes. Now I have a chance. Not just to better myself, but to make things better for every Negro in this country. If I'm successful, young Negro boys like you won't have to fight so hard. You won't have to put up with what my grandfather, my father, and I had to put up with. But if I fail . . ."

His voice trailed off. He looked like he had taken the weight of every African-American in the country on his shoulders.

"You won't fail," I assured Jackie. "You're going to be great."

"You sound pretty sure, Stosh."

I wasn't planning to tell Jackie or anybody else that I had come from the future. But as he stared at me with those piercing eyes, I felt compelled to tell the truth.

"Mr. Robinson," I said, taking a deep breath. "I know you're not going to believe this . . . but I come from the future."

"Excuse me?" Jackie asked, as if he might not have heard what I said.

"I traveled back in time more than fifty years to meet you."

"You did, eh?" Jackie chuckled, then went to look out the window. "Funny, I don't see your spaceship parked outside. I hope the police didn't tow it away."

"I didn't use a spaceship," I said, feeling a little angry that he was making fun of me. "I use baseball cards to travel through time."

"Baseball cards, you say?"

"Yeah. You see, I'm actually a white kid. I sort of turned black during the time travel procedure. I came here because I'm doing a report on you at school for Black History Month."

"Wait a minute," Jackie said, holding up one hand and clutching his stomach with the other. "I can accept that traveling through time may be possible. I may even be able to believe a white kid could turn black. But Black History Month?"

At that, Jackie let out a loud guffaw that woke the baby.

"You've got to be kidding! White kids from Kentucky studying *our* history? Now I *know* you're crazy!"

"You don't have to believe me," I told Jackie. "But because of people like you, there are going to be a lot of changes over the next fifty years. You're going to win the Rookie of the Year award this year. I'll bet you on that."

"That's a bet I'll take *any* day," Jackie said, thrusting out his hand to shake mine. "There's no such thing as a Rookie of the Year award!"

Jackie chuckled some more as he came over to tuck me in. "I like you, Stosh," he said. "Hey, do you want to go to the game tomorrow? You know, keep me company?"

"Sure!" I replied. "Who are you playing?"

"The Braves."

"Atlanta?"

Jackie looked at me with the same expression his wife had when I asked her the year. I realized instantly that there *were* no Atlanta Braves in 1947. The Braves played in Milwaukee before they moved to Atlanta.

"I mean Milwaukee," I quickly corrected myself. "The Milwaukee Braves."

Jackie kept staring at me, the same puzzled expression on his face. "I guess you don't follow baseball," he said.

Of course I do! Before they moved to Milwaukee, they were the *Boston* Braves! How could I be so dumb? I'd have to be a lot more careful in the future . . . and in the past.

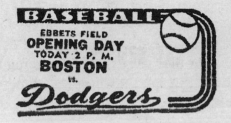

7

THE NEW BATBOY

I WOKE TO THE GENTLE SOUND OF JACKIE JR. SCREAMING his head off. Once the Robinsons calmed him down, we shared some cornflakes together and looked at the newspaper. The game wouldn't start until two o'clock, but Jackie wanted to get out to the ballpark early. Mrs. Robinson picked up Jackie Jr. and walked us outside. It was a cold, cloudy day.

"You should have brought a jacket," Mrs. Robinson told me.

Moms. They're all the same.

"I'll come out to the ballpark as soon as he wakes up from his nap," Mrs. Robinson said as she kissed Jackie good-bye. "You're going to be great, Jack."

"I know," he replied, gesturing toward me. "The kid already told me."

Jackie didn't have a car. We walked to the nearest subway stop. Jackie went through his pockets and came up with a couple of nickels. Five cents for a ride! Not bad. He gave me a nickel and we pushed our way through the turnstile.

The train wasn't crowded. There were about a dozen people sitting around us, most of them white. I didn't want to get into any trouble, so I tried not to make eye contact with anybody. A few people were staring at Jackie as he looked at a newspaper. I wasn't sure if it was because he was black, or because they knew he was one of the Dodgers.

He was nervous, he told me. He had played second base for the Montreal Royals in the minor leagues. But the Dodgers needed help at first and asked him to play that position. It would be a learning experience.

We had been on the subway for about fifteen minutes when Jackie told me we would be getting off at the next stop. The train screeched to a halt, and when the doors opened I could see a sign that said PROSPECT PARK/BOTANICAL GARDENS.

When we got out of the subway, Ebbets Field was nowhere in sight. The street sign said EMPIRE.

Jackie knew where to go, and I followed. We walked down Empire for a couple of blocks until we reached Bedford Avenue. We made a left at that corner. I looked up and saw the sign . . . EBBETS FIELD.

There it was. The mythical baseball shrine. It had been torn down long ago, I knew, but it existed for me. I was standing outside it. My heart beat faster.

There was a gas station across the street from the ballpark, and an automobile dealership next to it. They were selling DeSotos, a kind of car that I had never heard of.

There it was. The mythical baseball shrine. It had been torn
down long ago, but it existed for me. My heart beat faster.

There were no fans at the ballpark yet. Jackie led me through the center-field gate. We walked up a long ramp, which ended with a small opening. When we reached the opening, I could see the field for the first time.

New York had been a lot of concrete so far, so the overwhelming *greenness* of the field took me by surprise. It was a beautiful sight.

The ballpark actually seemed *smaller* than what I was expecting. The seats were really close to the field, so close that parts of the upper deck hung out over the playing field. Fans could look right down on the players.

The outfield walls were completely covered with advertising signs. VAN HEUSEN SHIRTS. EVER-READY SHAVING BRUSHES. BULOVA WATCHES. LIFEBUOY SOAP. BOTANY TIES. Guy products. A skinny horizontal sign read HIT SIGN WIN SUIT.

It looked like an impossible shot. The sign was only about four feet high and low to the ground, right behind where the rightfielder would be positioned.

The GEM RAZOR and ESQUIRE BOOT POLISH signs were against the right-field grass and leaning back slightly. The enormous scoreboard, with a big SCHAEFER BEER sign on it, stuck out about five feet into right center field. Playing the outfield with all those crazy angles must be a nightmare, I thought.

Jackie and I walked through a door marked CLUB-HOUSE: PLAYERS ONLY. The Dodger locker room was a big, rectangular room with a line of windows close to the ceiling. It was hot in there, and I didn't think it

The outfield walls were completely covered with advertising signs.

was because the air conditioning hadn't been turned on yet. The place *had* no air conditioning.

Lockers, each about the size of a phone booth, lined the walls. A clean uniform hung in each one. I scanned the names above the lockers—PEE WEE REESE . . . CARL FURILLO . . . DIXIE WALKER . . . PETE REISER . . . COOKIE LAVAGETTO . . . AL GIONFRIDDO. I knew these names from reading baseball books and hearing old stories.

Jackie found his locker. While he put on his uniform with the big 42 on its back, I took a walk around.

When I walked into the trainer's room, I was surprised to see a white kid about my age in there. He had his feet up on the massage table, and he was reading a magazine called *Amazing Stories*. The kid was wearing a Dodgers uniform.

"Whaddaya want?" he asked brusquely.

"Nothing," I replied.

"You the new batboy?"

"Uhh . . ." I certainly *wasn't* the new batboy. But he obviously didn't know that. And if the Dodgers needed a batboy, well, I figured, I can do that as well as anybody else. It could be kind of cool to be the batboy for the Brooklyn Dodgers.

"Yeah," I said, doing my best to look like I was telling the truth.

"Well, is you is or is you ain't?"

"I is!" I said more assertively. "I mean, I am. I'm the new batboy."

"I'm Anthony," the kid said. He didn't offer his

hand, so I didn't put mine out. "Call me Ant. Every-body does."

"Joe," I said. "Joe Stoshack."

"What's a colored boy doin' with a Polack name?"

"I don't know. My folks gave it to me."

I didn't like the Polack crack, but I had promised Mom I'd be on my best behavior, so I didn't slug him.

"How come you don't talk colored?"

"I talk the way I talk."

Ant looked me over, sizing me up. Usually when I meet new kids, they give me the benefit of the doubt. They don't hate me or like me yet, but they check me out to see if I'm okay. This Ant, I could tell, didn't like me the second he set eyes on me.

I had been careful to wear a plain old T-shirt and blue jeans so it wouldn't be obvious that I came from the future. But Ant was pretty observant.

"Where'd ya get dem dumb sneakers?" he asked.

I looked at my feet, then at Ant's. I was wearing a pair of Nikes, the cheapest ones they make. There was nothing fancy about them. I mean, they weren't Air Jordans or anything. But I guess my sneakers looked strange to Ant. He was wearing black canvas high tops. Their label said KEDS.

"I wore out my Keds," I said. "These are . . . new."

Ant took a uniform out of the closet and tossed it to me. It was heavy, much heavier than my Little League uniform. It must have been made of wool or flannel. The word *Dodgers* stretched across the chest, with the "Do" on one side of the buttons and "dgers" on the other.

I turned the uniform over to see what number I

JACKIE AND ME 47

had been given. I was hoping for something in the forties, like Jackie. But across the back of the uniform was the word BATBOY.

Ant led me back to the main clubhouse and pointed at the locker where I was supposed to change my clothes and stash my stuff. Jackie was sitting and reading some letters in front of his locker in the other corner.

As Ant walked away, he mumbled under his breath, "I can't believe I gotta work with a nigger."

I had heard the word before, but never directed toward *me*. The "N word" most people in my time call it. I knew it was about the worst word you could say to an African-American, though it never really meant much to me.

Now I felt angry and humiliated. Ant had already called me a Polack and now he was giving me the N word. The blood rushed to my face. Ant was on the other side of the clubhouse now, about to go into the trainer's room. I went after him. I was going to bust his face in.

I would have, too, but Jackie jumped up from his stool and grabbed me. Ant disappeared into the trainer's room.

"I'm gonna kill him!" I seethed.

"No you're not," Jackie said calmly.

"He called me a ni—" I couldn't even say the word.

"What, you've never heard that before?" Jackie burned his eyes into mine and poked a finger at my chest. "There will be *no* incidents, do you hear me? I made a promise to Mr. Rickey when he signed me. He said guys are going to say awful things to me.

Guys are going to *do* awful things to me. They're going to try to provoke me into fights. If I lose my temper and cause a riot or something, it will be ten, maybe twenty years before another Negro gets this chance. Understand?"

I didn't. Not entirely. "Did Mr. Rickey want a ballplayer who was afraid to fight back?" I asked.

"No," Jackie said. "He wanted a ballplayer with guts enough *not* to fight back."

Jackie went back to his mail and I put my uniform on. I stood in front of the mirror and looked at myself. The shirt was big on me, floppy all over. But so was Jackie's. That's just the way they wore them in 1947, I guessed. I still looked great. Like a Dodger. I was perfecting my batting stance in the mirror when I noticed Ant behind me.

"You ain't no player," he said, pointing a finger at me. "Let's get something straight. You're here to *serve* the players. You're just a batboy. I'm your boss. From now on, I want you to call me . . . Batman."

"Batman?" I asked. I couldn't help but laugh.

"Yeah, Batman," he replied. "What's so funny about that?"

"Nothing," I lied. At least he didn't insist on calling me Robin.

"Let's get to work," Ant said, hauling out some big boxes marked SPALDING. He opened the boxes and I could see there were hundreds of baseballs inside.

"What do we do with them, Batman?" I asked.

"What do you *think* we do with 'em?" he said, handing me a pen and a piece of paper. "This is Gionfriddo's signature. Copy it. And remember, two d's in Gionfriddo."

I looked at the piece of paper. It said "Al Gionfriddo" on it in smooth, flowing letters.

"The *batboys* autograph the balls?" I asked Ant incredulously. He looked at me as if I was stupid.

"Well, don't you think Al Gionfriddo has better things to do with his time than to sit around signing baseballs?"

Ant left again. I sat down at the table, picked up a ball, and began to write. *Al Gionfriddo*. I had never done this before. It's *hard* to write on a baseball, I realized right away. *Al Gionfriddo*. There isn't a lot of room between the seams. *Al Gionfriddo*. Worse, I was used to writing on a flat surface, so when I got to the "friddo" part and the ball curved down, my hand didn't move down with it. *Al Gionfriddo*.

I kept messing up, and fuming at Ant. He probably gave me the Gionfriddo baseballs because it was one of the longest names on the team. *Al Gionfriddo*. I remembered the name. In one of my baseball books back home, it said he was a little-known utility outfielder who became famous after he made one of the most spectacular catches in baseball history. *Al Gionfriddo*.

I was doing my best to control myself when another white kid walked into the clubhouse.

"I'm the new batboy," the kid said.

"The position has already been filled," I informed him.

"But over the phone somebody told me—"

"Try again next season," I suggested. The kid left dejectedly.

After I wrote *Al Gionfriddo* about a zillion times, my hand felt like a claw. As I was finishing up the last few Gionfriddos, Jackie sauntered by and looked over my shoulder.

"Nice handwriting." He chuckled. He said he was going to go out on the field and stretch a little.

I felt like plunging my hand into some ice water, but Ant showed up again. We got out the bats and balls, put clean towels in each locker and soap and shampoo in the showers.

"What about the batting helmets?" I asked Ant.

"Batting helmets?" He looked at me curiously.

They didn't *have* batting helmets in 1947.

"Where do you come from, Mars?" Ant asked with a mocking tone in his voice.

"Sorry," I said.

"You're pretty stupid, aren't you, boy?"

"No," I replied. I didn't think that telling him I got all As and one B on my last report card would do a lot of good.

"Oh yeah?" he challenged. "Can you read, boy? Can you spell cat?"

"C-A-T," I said.

"Hey, you're a regular genius! I bet you're so dumb, you don't even know who the President is."

The President? My mind raced. We learned all the presidents in school. I knew that the President during World War II was Franklin Roosevelt. But the war ended in 1945, and this was 1947. I scrambled to think of the presidents who followed Roosevelt. I wasn't sure of the order. Kennedy, Reagan, Nixon, Ford, Johnson, Bush, Eisenhower, Carter, Clinton, Truman . . .

"Truman," I guessed.

"Had to think about it, didn't you?" Ant smirked. "You *are* stupid."

At least I got the answer right. I breathed a sign of relief.

Ant looked like he was getting ready to humiliate me some more, but the Dodgers started drifting into the clubhouse.

"Hey, Pee Wee!" Ant shouted cheerily. "Dixie, Skoonj, we gonna go all the way this year?"

Ant knew all the players, and they all greeted him warmly. Everybody ignored me. I guess they were used to African-Americans doing things for them, so a black batboy wasn't any big deal. Ant didn't make any move to introduce me to anybody. I just went about my business, doing the chores he told me to do.

The clubhouse chatter was loud, funny, and dirty. I don't think I ever heard so many four-letter words before. The Dodgers seemed to be a really loose team, like one big happy family.

Jackie came in from the door leading to the dugout. Suddenly, all conversation stopped. I was pretty sure the other Dodgers had been introduced to Jackie during spring training, but maybe the reality of seeing him in their locker room on opening day threw them. Everybody stared at Jackie like he was an intruder. The silence was oppressive.

"Gentlemen." Jackie finally cleared his throat and announced, "As long as I have your attention, it seems like this would be a good time to make a short statement. Some of you may not like me because I'm a Negro. You certainly have the right to feel that way. I'm not concerned with your liking or disliking me. All I ask is that you respect me as a human being. Regardless of how you feel about me, I hope we can work together on the field. Thank you."

The players went back to their conversations, but more quietly. Some whispered among themselves. Nobody came over to talk to Jackie, and he didn't approach any of them.

I didn't know if the Dodgers felt the same way I did, but to me, tension was hanging over the clubhouse like a dark cloud. They no longer looked like a team; they looked like strangers getting ready for work.

I scanned the clubhouse while I swept the floor. Pee Wee Reese, the shortstop, was a little guy, but he looked like he was one of the team leaders. Carl Furillo, an outfielder, looked very serious. He was quietly rubbing something—it looked like a big bone—over the barrel of his bat over and over again. Hugh Casey, one of the relief pitchers, took a quick swig from a bottle of whiskey and then stashed it in his locker behind some other stuff.

An old white guy with glasses was sitting on top of a trunk sipping a Coke. I didn't know who he was, so I walked over to Jackie and asked him if somebody should kick the guy out of the clubhouse.

"That wouldn't be such a good idea," he replied, chuckling. "He's the manager of the team, Barney Shotton."

Dixie Walker, another outfielder, was sitting on a stool in front of his locker writing on a pad of paper. It must be a letter to his mother or his wife, I guessed.

My dad had a Dixie Walker baseball card in his collection, so I knew a little about him. He was a great hitter, that was for sure. He led the National League with a .357 average in 1944. Dixie's dad and his uncle both played in the big leagues before him. And his younger brother Harry was a star for the St. Louis Cardinals.

Dixie finished what he was writing, and he walked over to Hugh Casey's locker. Walker whispered something to Casey, showed him the pad of paper and handed him the pen. Casey read what was written on the paper and signed it.

Whatever Dixie wrote on the paper, it wasn't a letter to his mom. I was curious.

Walker then went over to Bobby Bragan, who was strapping on some catcher's gear. Bragan listened to what Dixie had to say, and he signed the paper too. It must be some kind of a petition or something, I gathered.

Next, Dixie came over to Eddie Stanky's locker. Stanky, I knew, played second base for the Dodgers. When Dixie handed him the pen to sign, Stanky shook his head no and walked away. That was odd.

As players were starting to file out of the clubhouse to warm up on the field, Pee Wee Reese approached Dixie and asked to see the pad. Dixie handed it to him and Reese read it. He looked at Walker, said a few words, and then he tore off the top sheet of paper and ripped it in half. Reese threw the two pieces in a trash can and walked out of the clubhouse.

Hmmm. I was dying to know what was on the paper. I waited until all the players had left the clubhouse, and then I reached into the trash and fished it out.

This is what it said . . .

We, the undersigned players of the Brooklyn Dodgers, agree that we wish to be traded rather than take the field with a colored man on our team.

Underneath that, there were the signatures of Dixie Walker, Bobby Bragan, and a few other players.

I thought about saving the paper for my collection of baseball memorabilia back home. Those autographs would be worth a lot of money someday. But I decided they were guys I didn't want to have in my collection. I crumpled up the paper and tossed it back in the trash.

8

EBBETS FIELD

THE DELICIOUS SMELL OF ROASTED PEANUTS HIT ME AS soon as I walked out on the field. Fans were entering the ballpark now, the early birds who loved the game so much they had to watch batting practice. Ant told me we didn't have much to do until the game started, so I should just hang around and get the players anything they might need.

"The tickets for forthcoming games will be sold in the marble rotunda," boomed the public address announcer.

All the Dodgers were playing catch, loosening up their arms. I was close enough to see the sweat on their faces. They seemed to throw the ball so effortlessly and so accurately. Baseballs were exploding into gloves with a wonderful popping noise, like firecrackers set off one after the other.

"Hey Stosh, warm me up."

It was Jackie, standing around looking uncomfortable. While each of the other Dodgers was playing catch with a teammate, nobody invited Jackie to join them.

My throwing hand was killing me from signing Al Gionfriddo's name on all those baseballs, but I wasn't about to turn down the chance to play catch with Jackie Robinson. He flipped me a glove and I dashed out near the third-base line. The glove, I noticed, was much smaller than the one I had at home. It had hardly any padding or webbing.

Jackie whipped the ball to me. I had played a lot of baseball in my life, but with *kids*. Jackie's throw came at me so fast I was afraid it was going to hit me in the head. Awkwardly, I stuck the glove in front of my face just in time. The ball smacked into the palm of my hand.

It must have been some kind of involuntary response, but tears gathered in my eyes. My hand hurt so much I thought it was going to come off at the wrist. Now *both* of my hands were killing me.

I didn't want anyone to know the pain I was in, so I pretended it didn't hurt. I reared back and threw the ball to Jackie as hard as I could. The ball went sailing over his head. Jackie laughed and chased it down.

"Easy!" he yelled. "Nice and easy."

After a few throws, I got used to how hard Jackie threw. Some kids along the left-field stands were watching us, and I felt like turning around and shouting at them, "Hey losers! I bet you wish you were me! I'm playing catch with Jackie Robinson!"

I discovered that if I moved my hand backward slightly at the moment the ball hit my glove, it cushioned the impact a little. But even so, when Jackie told me he was going to go run a few wind sprints in the outfield, it was a relief. My hand was throbbing, but otherwise I felt great. I couldn't wait to tell my dad about it.

"A little boy has been found lost," the public address announcer informed the crowd.

The stands were filling up as game time approached. There was the sound of a cowbell clanging. When I looked to see where it was coming from, I spotted a fat lady with stringy gray hair swinging the cowbell over her head. "Home wuz never like dis, mac!" she shouted in a raspy voice that could be could heard all over the ballpark.

"Butterfly girl in section twenty-three!" Eddie Stanky announced. All the Dodgers turned around to peer up into the stands.

"What's a butterfly girl?" I asked.

"A butterfly girl," Stanky informed me, "is a girl who's so pretty that just looking at her gives you butterflies."

In the first-base stands, a bunch of guys with a tuba, saxophone, and other musical instruments were playing. They sounded terrible, but nobody seemed to mind. It said DODGER'S SYM-PHONY BAND on their bass drum. When the three umpires came out on the field, the band launched into "Three Blind Mice." Everybody laughed, including the umps.

There was no Dodger mascot. Nobody was paid to dress up like a chicken and entertain the fans. The fans entertained themselves.

The public address announcer boomed, "Will the

fans along the outfield railing please remove their clothing?" There was scattered laughter. I wasn't sure if it was a joke or not. But the people sitting along the outfield fence *did* take their coats off the railing.

Most of the Dodgers went out along the first-base line to shake hands, sign autographs, and chat with the fans. Jackie, hesitant, lingered near the dugout. He was scanning the crowd, looking for his wife, I guessed. Hundreds of African-American fans gathered around him.

They looked different from the white fans. It wasn't just skin color. They had a look in their eyes. Worship, some of them. Pride, others. Just plain old happiness in some cases.

The men were dressed in suits and ties. The women were wearing fancy dresses and jewelry. They had dressed up like they were going to church. An old man kept shaking his head back and forth. He must have never thought the day would come when an African-American would be a part of what was always called the National Pastime.

Dozens of people gathered around, handing Jackie things for him to sign. I saw a little black boy hand Jackie a scorecard. The kid was so awestruck, he couldn't even get the words out to ask for an autograph. He just stared with his mouth open, like Jackie was a god or something.

The Braves took the field to warm up and the Dodgers gathered in the dugout. Jackie sat in the corner by himself. I was going to go sit next to him, but Dixie Walker motioned me over to him.

"Hey kid," he said, pulling a dollar out of his pocket

Most of the Dodgers went out along the first-base line to shake hands, sign autographs, and chat with the fans. Jackie, hesitant, lingered near the dugout.

and handing it to me, "go get me a hot dog, will ya? Everything on it."

I took the bill and went up into the stands until I found a hot dog vendor. He was taking care of a lady with a baby. When she turned around, I recognized her.

"Mrs. Robinson!" I said.

"Jackie took a long nap," she said, shifting Jackie Jr. from one hip to the other, "and then I couldn't find a cab driver who would stop and pick us up."

"You need me to help you get a hot dog?" I asked.

"No, I hate hot dogs," she replied.

The hot dog vendor reached into his cart with his tongs and pulled out a baby bottle.

"That should be warm enough," he told her. She thanked the vendor and gave the bottle to Jackie Jr.

"I'm glad to see they put you to work," Mrs. Robinson said before going to her seat. "Joe, after the game I need to talk to you about something."

I fished the dollar out of my pocket and ordered a hot dog with everything on it. I was afraid a dollar wouldn't be enough, but the vendor gave me the dog and handed me ninety cents.

I rushed back to the dugout. When I gave Dixie Walker the hot dog and the change, he handed the change back to me. That's a ninety-cent tip on a ten-cent hot dog, I figured. Not bad! Maybe Dixie wasn't such a terrible guy after all.

"Mr. Walker," I said, "can I ask you a question?"

"Sure, kid."

"What do you have against Jackie Robinson?"

Dixie looked at me, then he looked around, as if

he didn't want everyone to hear what he was about to say.

"Son," he said, lowering his voice, "I got nothin' against Robinson or any of you Negroes. Ya gotta understand, though. I come from Alabama. And where I come from, a pig and a chicken don't live in the same pen. They'd kill each other. Ya keep everything separate and everyone's happy. That's just the way nature works. That's the way it's always been. That's the way it *should* be. Same thing with white folks and you Negroes. It's nothin' personal, mind you."

I certainly didn't agree, but I wasn't in a position to argue with him. Both teams were starting to line up on the foul lines. A microphone was brought out to home plate and a bunch of guys in Army uniforms gathered around it.

"Oh say can you see . . ."

The players quickly removed their caps and held them over their hearts. Jackie was standing next to Bobby Bragan and a pitcher named Kirby Higbe, but when they realized it, they moved a few feet away from him. That left Carl Furillo closer to Jackie, and he moved away, too.

I couldn't take my eyes off Jackie. I felt sure he was going to raise a fist in the air, or spit, or perform some act of defiance. He didn't. His act of defiance was just being there. He stood off to the side, solemnly, alone, while the rest of the Dodgers stood together as a unit.

"O'er the land of the free . . . and the home of the brave."

9

OPENING DAY

"PLAY BALL!" SHOUTED THE UMPIRE.

Pee Wee Reese, at the edge of the dugout, waved his arm and the Dodgers sprinted to their positions. Reese at shortstop. Spider Jorgenson at third. Eddie Stanky at second. Joe Hatten was pitching, with Bruce Edwards behind the plate. The outfield, from left to right, was patrolled by Gene Hermanski, Pete Reiser, and Dixie Walker. And, of course, Jackie trotted out to first base.

It had happened. A black man had entered the white man's game. When Jackie stepped across the first-base line, the color barrier crashed to the ground. And I had the best seat in the house.

"Hum that pea, baby!" somebody shouted to Joe Hatten.

Hatten, a lefthander, retired the Braves easily in the first. When Jackie trotted off the field, I told him that Rachel had arrived with Jackie Jr. He seemed relieved.

Ant told me to kneel in the on-deck circle and re-
trieve the bat after any of the Dodgers hit the ball.
He would chase foul balls behind the plate and supply
the umpire with fresh baseballs if they were needed.

Eddie Stanky walked up to the plate to lead off for
the Dodgers. Some of the guys on the team called him
"Brat." On the mound for Boston was Johnny Sain,
a righthander who'd won twenty games in the last
season. I knew the name. Sain and Warren Spahn
were the only decent pitchers Boston had, which led
to a famous baseball rhyme: "Spahn and Sain, then
pray for rain."

"Rip it, Brat!" somebody called from the stands.

As Stanky worked the count to two balls and a
strike, a loud cheer went up from the stands. I turned
around and saw Jackie coming out to the on-deck
circle. The black fans—and there were a lot of them—
were yelling their heads off.

"What's he throwing, Stosh?" Jackie asked me as
he loosened up, swinging three bats.

"Curveballs," I replied. "All curves."

Stanky flied out to right field. It was Jackie's turn
to bat, his first in the majors.

A roar went up in the stands as Jackie tossed away
two of the bats and walked slowly toward the plate.
Every black person in Ebbets Field was standing, and
most of the whites were, too. The players in both dug-
outs moved to the edge of the bench.

I didn't hear any racist comments, but that doesn't
mean there weren't any. There were a few scattered
boos, but for the most part, the Brooklyn fans were

on Jackie's side. His skin color didn't seem to matter. The color of his uniform did.

There was no electronic scoreboard instructing people to GET LOUD! or LET'S HEAR SOME NOISE. It wasn't necessary. I put my fingers in my ears to shut out some of the noise.

Sain waited for the sound to die down a little before he looked in for the sign.

"Ten bucks says Sain makes him eat dirt," I heard somebody in the Dodger dugout say.

"Twenty," somebody else countered.

Jackie dug his back foot into the outside line of the batter's box. He took a deep breath and held both arms extended far away from his body. He gripped the handle of the bat high, at eye level, and pumped the bat back and forth as Sain wound up. Jackie quickly took his left hand off his bat, wiped it on his pants leg, and gripped the bat again.

It was a curveball, just off the outside corner. Sain, it appeared, was no headhunter. He was going to pitch to Jackie just like he'd pitch to anybody else.

Jackie and Sain battled until Sain put a fastball over the inside part of the plate. Jackie took a swing at it, a choppy, lunging swing. He smacked a grounder to short.

Jackie broke from the batter's box like a bullet. The shortstop scooped the ball up and hurried his throw to first base. Jackie stepped on the bag at about the same time as the ball hit the first baseman's mitt.

"Yer out!" the umpire yelled, jerking his thumb up.

He looked safe to me, but Dodger manager Barney

Jackie dug his back foot into the outside line of the batter's box. He took a deep breath and held both arms extended far away from his body.

Shotton didn't complain. Jackie tossed a look at the ump, but he didn't argue the call.

Jackie made an out, but the black fans roared with approval anyway. It didn't matter to them that Jackie didn't get a hit. What mattered most was that he was given the *opportunity* to get a hit.

Pete Reiser drew a walk, but Dixie Walker flied out to end the inning. No score.

After the first inning, the crowd settled down. The color barrier had been broken. The earth didn't spin off its axis. The world as we knew it didn't cease to exist. It was like any other baseball game.

The Dodgers scored a run in the third inning on a ground ball out. Boston tied it up in the fifth, then scored twice more in the sixth. Jackie wasn't Superman. He flied to left in the third and bounced into a rally-killing double play in the fifth.

In the seventh inning, Stanky led off with a walk. Jackie dropped down a perfect bunt to advance the runner, and the throw to first hit him on the shoulder. As the ball bounded into right field, both runners advanced. The letter *E* on the big Schaefer Beer sign lit up to indicate an error had been made.

Pete Reiser followed with a double off Johnny Sain that landed just inside the right-field foul line. Stanky and Jackie both scored.

As Jackie crossed the plate, I put my hand up for a high five. He put his hand down for me to shake it. We missed hands. He must have thought I was a real idiot.

Reiser would also eventually come home, and the

Dodgers ended up winning the game by the score of 5–3.

When the final out was made, the lady in center field clanged her cowbell and shouted, "Eacha hearts out, ya bums!"

Barney Shotton gave each of the Dodgers a pat on the back as they filed into the clubhouse. They tore off their uniforms and threw them into a pile in the middle of the floor.

Most of the players hung around for a while, going over the game, but Jackie showered and dressed quickly. None of the players congratulated him for making history.

"I have to go out a special exit," Jackie whispered to me. "They're afraid the crowds might get out of control if they see me. Can you find your way back to the hotel?"

I told him I could, and he slipped me a nickel for the subway.

It had been a long day and I was tired. I was also anxious to go out on the street and see if I could get some baseball cards for my dad.

"Not so fast, black boy," Ant said when he saw me heading for the door. "The game ain't over for *us* yet."

For batboys, I learned, most of the work comes *after* the ninth inning. There were uniforms to bag up for the laundry. The dugout had to be mopped clean of tobacco juice. The clubhouse had to be swept and mopped. Equipment had to be cleaned and put away.

Ant had me do most of the dirty work, while he sat

there with his feet up on a table. He seemed to enjoy watching me.

"I'm sure you know how to shine shoes," Ant smirked, just when I thought my work was done. "I'll take half and you take half."

He had lined up thirty pairs of cleats on the floor. One pair for each player, plus all the coaches. My right hand was killing me from signing all those fake autographs. My left hand was killing me from catching Jackie's warmup throws. And now I would have to shine shoes! I wished I was back in Louisville, soaking in the bathtub.

"You're lucky," Ant informed me. "The polish won't even show up on your skin."

I started polishing, doing my best to ignore Ant's remark. By the time I finished shining the fifth pair, I was dragging. But Ant was already on his sixth pair, so I worked a little faster.

Neither of us said out loud that we were racing, but I think we both knew we were. Ant kept looking over at me to see how many pairs I had finished. I did the same to him. He seemed surprised that I was able to keep up with him.

It was uncomfortable, the two of us alone in the clubhouse together. I guess Ant felt it, too. I don't think he had ever spent so much time with a black person. At first he didn't say anything to me, but after a while he pulled the *Amazing Stories* magazine out of his back pocket.

"Ya hear 'bout dis?" he asked, showing me an article. "Last month sump'n fell outta da sky in Roswell, New Mexico. Dey think it might be aliens or sump'n."

"I heard about it," I replied. "I'll believe it when I see it."

"Oh I believe it right now," Ant said, looking me straight in the eye. "Aliens are here. No doubt about it."

By the tenth pair of shoes, I was wiped out. But Ant saw me catching up to him, so he cranked it up a little faster. He was still one pair ahead of me. By the time I got to the fifteenth pair, I decided I would never wear leather shoes again for the rest of my life. I had nearly caught up, and we were both working on the last pair at the same time.

"Done!" Ant said triumphantly just a few seconds before I finished the last shoe. We both wiped our faces with towels.

"Here, kid," he said, pulling three dollar bills from his pocket and handing them to me. "Your pay."

"Thanks . . . Batman."

I didn't know that batboys got paid. I accepted the money gratefully. I could use it to buy more baseball cards for my dad.

Ant and I had come to an understanding, I felt. He didn't like me very much. I didn't like him very much. But we both had a job to do, so we did it.

"Be here tomorrow at ten o'clock sharp," he said as we left the clubhouse. He locked the door behind us and walked out the exit without saying good-bye.

10

THE STREETS OF FLATBUSH

IT HAD BEEN COOL GOING BACK IN TIME TO MEET JACKIE Robinson. I had enough information to do my report. I was exhausted. All I wanted to do was go back home to Louisville and fall into my bed.

But I couldn't do that. Not yet, anyway. Dad had given me an assignment. I had to at least *try* to carry it out.

I had to find a baseball card store. My plan was to buy as many cards as I could carry. Then I would go back to Jackie Robinson's hotel. In the middle of the night, I would use my Ken Griffey Jr. card to take me and my old cards to the future.

It was about five o'clock in the afternoon when I left Ebbets Field. I started wandering around the streets looking for a baseball card store. Brooklyn didn't look anything like Louisville. It didn't look anything like Manhattan either.

The street was filled with people, almost all white people. Old guys in undershirts sitting on lawn chairs. Women gathered in clusters, gabbing in Italian, German, and Irish accents. I didn't see any black people, and I had the sense that the white people on the street were staring at me.

Vendors pushed carts down the street. One guy was selling corn on the cob from a big basket he attached to his bike. Another came around sharpening knives and scissors. There wasn't a baseball card store in sight.

Kids were everywhere. Girls playing hopscotch, roller skating, jumping rope. Boys pitching pennies, flicking yo-yos, playing dominoes, marbles, and games I'd never seen before. Back home in Louisville, most of the games I played with my friends were video games.

It was so noisy! Radios blared out of every window. Trolleys clanged and screeched around the corners. There was a siren somewhere, but nobody paid attention to it. Moms were leaning out their windows, calling their kids to come home and eat. I could hear somebody practicing scales on a violin.

There was a bell in the distance and all the kids started yelling, "G'Jooma! G'Jooma!" I couldn't imagine what that meant. But a minute later, a Good Humor truck arrived and it all became clear. My eyes were wide open. It was all very new and different to me.

A group of shirtless boys were down the street playing stickball. Now *this* was a game I knew. In fact, back in Louisville, I *ruled* at stickball. I leaned up against a fence to watch them.

For a bat, the kids were using a sawed-off broom handle with black tape around the lower half. The ball was an old tennis ball, hard and dead. They had drawn a scoreboard with chalk in the street.

"Wanna play?"

The kid who said that was looking toward me, but I figured he must have been talking to somebody else. I turned around to see if anybody was behind me.

"*You*," the kid said. "Colored boy. Wanna play?"

"Uh . . . okay."

I came around to the other side of the fence, and all the kids in the game jogged in from their positions.

"Hey, I ain't playin' with no nigger!" one of the kids said.

"Shut up, Louie!" said another. I stood there awkwardly, pretending I didn't care if they let me play or not.

"The Dodgers got a colored guy now," a third kid said. "If it's okay with the Bums, it's okay with me."

"Me too."

"Fuhgetaboutit," the kid they called Louie said, picking his shirt up off the ground. "I'm goin' home."

"Okay," the biggest kid said. "You can play."

They explained the ground rules to me. Home plate was a manhole cover. Trees on each side of the street were first and third base. Some kid's shirt lying on the ground was second base. A ball hit past one sewer was a single. Two sewers was a double. Three sewers, well, nobody could hit a ball that far.

"Ya hit it past the Chevy on a fly, it's a double," a kid explained. "Ya hit past the Ford, it's a triple."

They assigned me to the team at bat. Everybody ran to their positions. A kid on my team picked up the bat and wiggled it around.

"Look, I'm Pee Wee Reese!" he boasted.

"You look more like Rizzuto, Alphonse!" somebody yelled. "And he stinks!"

The pitcher went into his windup, and the kid who was imitating Reese took a big swing at the ball. He dribbled an easy roller back to the pitcher for an out. Somebody told me it was my turn to hit.

I grabbed the bat and walked up to the manhole cover. The broom was longer and thinner than anything I ever swung. I didn't want to make a fool of myself. I pumped the broom back and forth a few times.

"Hey look!" somebody yelled. "It's Jackie Robinson!" Everybody laughed.

The pitcher went into his windup and tossed the tennis ball. It looked hittable and I whipped the broom handle around. I could tell right away I got all of it.

"Could be three sewers!" somebody yelled.

The ball was up high, curving to the left, toward an apartment building. As it came down, somebody said, "Uh-oh!"

The ball crashed against a window and shattered it. For a second, I just froze. I just stood there with the bat in my hand, admiring my home run.

"That was a twenty-five-cent ball!" complained one of the kids.

"You hooligans!" a lady screamed through the broken window. "I'm gonna call the cops on you!"

"Run for it!" one of the kids yelled. Instantly, they all dashed away, like roaches after somebody turned the light on.

I took off at top speed and ducked around the first corner. After I had gone a couple of blocks and saw that nobody was chasing me, I slowed down and tried to act casual. If the lady told the police it was a black kid, it would be hard to hide. I didn't hear any sirens, and relaxed a little.

Stores lining the street were selling just about everything anybody would want to buy, it seemed. Fish. Newspapers. Pots and pans. Radios. Everything but baseball cards. I fished a dime out of my pocket and bought a hot dog from a street vendor.

I noticed four kids kneeling on a corner. They were throwing something against a wall. As I got closer, I could see that they were flipping baseball cards.

My dad told me he not only flipped cards when he was a kid, but he even put them in the spokes of his bike with a clothespin to make a noise like a motor. Incredible! Some of those cards would be worth hundreds of dollars. If these kids were smart, they'd put them in plastic pages instead of throwing them at a wall. But they didn't have a clue.

"Excuse me," I asked one of the kids, "is there a baseball card store in this neighborhood?"

The kids looked at me oddly, and then at each other. I wasn't sure if it was because of what I said or because they weren't used to seeing black kids in their neighborhood.

"Go back to Harlem, jungle bunny," one of the kids said.

"Yeah, beat it," said another.

They had me outnumbered four to one. I wasn't about to pick a fight.

"Look," I said as politely as possible, "I don't want any trouble. I just want to know if there's a store around here that sells baseball cards."

"A *what*?" asked one of them, a kid who hadn't spoken before. He seemed nicer than his friends.

"A store that sells baseball cards."

"Bubblegum cards?" asked the kid. "Try the grocery on the corner of Flatbush Avenue. He might have some."

The kid looked familiar to me somehow, but I couldn't place him.

"Your turn, Flip," somebody urged the kid.

"Flip?" I asked. "Your last name. It's not—"

"Valentini," he replied. "What's it to ya?"

Flip Valentini! I had traveled back over fifty years and who should I meet up with but the guy who lent me the Jackie Robinson card . . . as a kid! The world was a strange place.

"Let me give you a piece of advice," I told Flip Valentini. "Keep your bubblegum cards in a safe place. When you get older and you move out of your mom's house, take 'em with you. Whatever you do, don't let her throw them away."

Flip looked at me like I was nuts and went back to his game. I bought another hot dog from a vendor and headed for the grocery store Flip told me about.

The sign on the front of the store said ITALIAN & AMERI-
CAN GROCERIES. SAM HERSKOWITZ.

Before opening the door, I hesitated. I knew that
black people and white people used to have to use
separate restaurants, separate hotels, even separate
water fountains. Maybe I wouldn't be allowed in this
store. But there was no sign on the door saying I
couldn't come in, so I opened it.

There was a man standing behind the counter, wiping it with a rag. I looked around the store. He sold
a little bit of everything. Man, if only I could buy up
all this stuff and save it for fifty years, I thought, I'd
be rich.

"Do you serve colored people here?" I asked.

I wasn't exactly sure how to word that. When I was
younger, we used the word *black,* but as I grew older
it became *African-American.* Jackie Robinson, I noticed, referred to himself as a Negro. And white people in his time, when they weren't using the *N* word
or some other mean word, usually said *colored.* It
was confusing.

"There's only one kind of people I don't serve, son."

"Who?" I asked.

"Giants fans," he replied. "You're not one of *them,*
are you?"

"Oh no," I said, "I'm for the Dodgers all the way."

"Good boy. So what can I do for ya?"

"I want to buy some . . . bubblegum cards."

He looked at me like I had told him I wanted to
buy some elephants.

"Are you meshuga?" he asked.

I didn't know what that meant, so I didn't say anything.

"Are you crazy?" he translated. "I don't *sell* bubble-gum cards, son."

I was about to turn around and walk out, but he reached under the counter and handed me a pack of cards.

"I *give* 'em away."

"You *give* them away?" I asked, astonished. "Why?"

"Where are you from, son? Companies give 'em to me with their products. As promotions. To get people to buy stuff, y'know. I couldn't sell 'em."

"Do you have any more I could keep?"

"Whaddaya want 'em for so bad?" he asked, checking under the counter.

"I'm a collector," I replied.

"Garbage collector," the man mumbled to himself. He scooped up a few more packs and handed them to me.

The door jingled open and a heavy-set delivery man came in. He was wheeling a dolly stacked with bread. On the back of his uniform was the word *Bond*. At first, I didn't make the connection.

"Where should I put these, Mr. Herskowitz?" the Bond bread guy asked.

Mr. Herskowitz directed him to put the bread in the corner of the store. They both signed some papers. The Bond guy was about to leave when he stopped and turned around.

"Oh, I almost forgot. You want any of these, Mr. Herskowitz? They told me to clear 'em out of the warehouse."

He held out a pack of baseball cards. *Jackie Robinson cards.*

Bond Bread! That was the company that put out the Jackie Robinson card I used to travel back to 1947!

There were thirteen cards in that pack, I knew. It would sell for five thousand dollars back home. My eyes must have bugged out of my head.

"No thanks," said Mr. Herskowitz, "but I bet this young man would take them off your hands."

"Here, kid."

The Bond guy flipped me the pack of cards. I missed it, but scooped it off the floor like it was a gold nugget.

"How many of these do you have in the warehouse?" I asked desperately.

"A few hundred, I guess," he replied. "There are just stacks and stacks of 'em. Why? You want 'em?"

Want them? I did a quick mental calculation. If one pack was worth five thousand dollars, ten packs would be worth fifty thousand dollars. A hundred packs would be worth . . . a half a million dollars. Two hundred packs . . .

I started to feel dizzy. Dad would go meshuga when I showed up back home and handed him his suitcase with a million dollars' worth of baseball cards in it!

"I want them!" I said, my voice cracking a little.

"Meet me back here first thing Thursday morning," the Bond guy said. "I'll bring you everything I got."

"Can I go to the warehouse with you right now and pick them up?" I asked hopefully.

"It's closed for the day," he informed me, "and I

gotta deliver all over the city between now and Wednesday. Just meet me back here on Thursday morning and I'll take care of you."

I thanked the Bond guy about ten times before he left.

"You must really love baseball cards," Mr. Herskowitz commented.

"I do," I said, turning to leave. "By the way, you wouldn't have any Mickey Mantle cards lying around, would you?"

"Mickey *who*?"

"Forget it," I said, and closed the door behind me with a jingle.

11

FIGHTING BACK

I WAS ON CLOUD NINE. I HAD MET THE GREAT JACKIE Robinson, just as I'd hoped to. I had been to Ebbets Field, and I even was a batboy for the Brooklyn Dodgers. To top it all off, soon I would have a million dollars' worth of baseball cards.

It doesn't get much better than this, I thought as I rode the subway back to Jackie Robinson's hotel.

Of course, I was going to have to change my time travel plans a little. I couldn't go home right away. I would have to stay in 1947 until Thursday to get the baseball cards from the Bond Bread guy.

But that was okay. I knew from the last time that no matter how long I stayed in the past, I would return home and wake up in my bed the morning after I left.

The New York Giants and Philadelphia Phillies were coming into town. I could batboy for the Dodgers for a few days, get the baseball cards on Thursday morning, and then go home.

*   *   *

By the time I reached the McAlpin Hotel, it was dark outside. Mrs. Robinson was doing the dinner dishes when I knocked on the door. Jackie was playing peek-a-boo with Jackie Jr., trying to get him to stop crying, but it wasn't working very well.

"Joe, we need to talk," Mrs. Robinson said seriously as I greeted them. "I tried to track down your mama. There's nobody named Stoshack in Louisville, Kentucky. We need to know your real name and where you really live."

"I can explain," I said, "My real name *is* Joe Stoshack. I live in Louisville, Kentucky, and I know it's hard for you to believe this, but it's the truth. I went back in time to get here. I live fifty years into the future. That's why you couldn't find my mom. She's not *there* yet."

Mrs. Robinson looked at Jackie, then held the back of her hand against my forehead. That's what Mom does when she's checking to see if I have a fever.

"Jack," she said finally, "I think we should call the police."

"Don't call the police!" I begged. "I didn't do anything wrong."

"You expect us to believe that you traveled through time?"

"I don't expect you to believe it," I said sadly. "But it's true."

"Ease up on the boy, Rae," Jackie said. "He's a good kid."

"Can I please stay with you until Thursday?" I asked. "Then I'll go back home. Promise."

Mrs. Robinson didn't have much fight in her. It was late. She was tired. The dishes weren't done. Jackie was upset because he'd gone hitless on opening day. Jackie Jr. was upset because, well, because he was five months old and babies get upset for no particular reason.

"Thursday?" Mrs. Robinson asked wearily.

"After that you'll never see me again," I said honestly.

"Okay, you can stay," she said, putting the sheets on the couch for me. "But I don't believe a word of that future stuff."

The Dodgers beat the Braves again the next day, 13-6. Jackie didn't get good wood on the ball. He was pressing. It was obvious. He was nervous, anxious, and swinging at bad pitches.

The next two games were against the New York Giants at the Polo Grounds. The Dodgers lost both— 10-4 and 4-3. Jackie didn't help much.

I was getting pretty good at being a batboy, though. I had learned the routine, which made everything a lot easier. After one of the Giants games, I even beat Ant in the daily shoeshine race.

As if things weren't tough enough for Jackie, all kinds of rumors were swirling around. I heard some whispers around the clubhouse that he wasn't as good as the players expected him to be. Some newspaper articles said he might be sent down to the minor leagues for more "seasoning."

The St. Louis Cardinals—led by Dixie Walker's brother Harry—were rumored to be planning a strike if Jackie took the field against them. On the Dodgers, the players were cordial toward Jackie, but certainly not friendly. Nobody invited Jackie out to dinner after a game. Nobody sat next to him or told him jokes. He didn't join in the clubhouse card games. He was alone.

The first road trip of the season was coming up, and word was passed around that the Dodgers wouldn't be staying at their usual hotel in Philadelphia—the Benjamin Franklin. Negroes weren't allowed there. The team would stay at the Warwick Hotel instead. Even at the Warwick, Jackie wouldn't be allowed to eat his meals in the main dining hall with the rest of the team. He would have to eat in his room. And Philadelphia was called "The City of Brotherly Love!"

Then there were the threats. Part of my job was to go through fan mail, sort it, and put it in each player's locker. Nuts wrote to Jackie every day saying they were going to kill him. Somebody wrote that Jackie would be shot if he crossed the foul line to take the field the next day. There were threats to assault Rachel, to kidnap Jackie Jr.

"Don't tell Rachel," Jackie said simply as he handed me this:

Every time he stepped out of the dugout, Jackie looked up into the stands defiantly. It was as if he were *daring* somebody to take a shot at him.

Jackie pretended that the pressure didn't bother him, but I could tell it did. It showed in his hitting. He was in a deep slump.

I got up extra early Thursday morning. The Robinsons were still sleeping. I threw on my clothes, grabbed my dad's empty suitcase, and hopped on the subway to Brooklyn.

The grocery store was closed when I arrived, but it wasn't long before Mr. Herskowitz arrived and unlocked the door. The Bond truck pulled up shortly after. The delivery man hauled his bread out.

"You're here bright and early," he said cheerfully as he rolled his hand truck into the store.

"Did you bring the bubblegum cards?" I asked anxiously.

"Yup," he replied "Lucky I got 'em, too, because my boss was about to throw 'em in the incinerator."

He went back to the truck and brought out a large cardboard box. I pulled open the flaps and there they were—hundreds of packs, easy, of brand new, never opened, mint condition, 1947 Bond Bread Jackie Robinson baseball cards!

It took my breath away. I felt my heart beating furiously, and my forehead began to sweat. This must be what it felt like to the guy who started the gold rush in California, I thought. I thanked the Bond guy over and over again as I poured the packs of cards into my dad's suitcase.

As he climbed back in his truck, I walked over and handed him one of the packs of cards.

"You're going to think this is crazy, but save this," I told him. "Give it to your kids. Tell them to pass it on it to *their* kids."

"Why?" the guy asked.

"You wouldn't believe me if I told you," I said.

"Okay, kid," he shrugged, slipping the pack into his shirt pocket as he put the truck into gear.

I had over a million dollars' worth of cards in my suitcase. I could have taken the subway back to the Robinsons' place and zapped myself back to the future with my treasure. But I was only a few blocks from Ebbets Field. The Dodgers would be hosting the Philadelphia Phillies at two o'clock. I decided to stash the suitcase in the back of Jackie's locker and work one last game before going home.

The Phillies have always been pretty terrible, I knew that. In over a hundred years they won the World Series only *once,* in 1980. That's pathetic.

But the Phils started the 1947 season pretty well, winning four of their first six games. They were in second place in the National League, just ahead of Brooklyn.

As the Dodgers took the field in the first inning, Phillies manager Ben Chapman rose to the top of the dugout step. I saw him cup his hands around his mouth and holler, "Hey nigger! Why don't you go back to the cotton field where you belong?"

Other teams had razzed Jackie from the bench, but no more than they razzed the other Dodgers. For the most part, they kept the N word out of it. This was different. There was a hostility coming from Chapman that went beyond the usual baseball bench jockeying. This was pure hatred.

The rest of the Phillies, taking their cue from their manager, joined in.

"They're waiting for you in the jungles, black boy!"

"Hey snowflake, want some watermelon?"

"We don't want you here, brownie!"

Their voices could be heard clearly in the Dodger dugout, which meant they could also be heard in the stands. The umpires didn't do anything about it. The Dodger bench was like a tomb. Everybody looked embarrassed.

At first base, Jackie didn't make a peep. But he looked like a teapot just before it comes to a boil.

Ralph Branca was the Dodgers' starting pitcher. He was a young guy, about twenty-one. He threw hard.

Branca got the Phillie leadoff batter to slap a grounder to short. Pee Wee Reese scooped up the ball and threw it to Jackie at first base in time to get the out. But the batter didn't step on the right side of first base, like you're supposed to. Instead, he aimed his foot for the left side, the side where Jackie's foot touched the bag. The hitter's spikes caught Jackie above the ankle. He crumpled to the ground like he'd been shot.

I was sure Jackie was hurt bad and would leave the game. But he didn't lie there. He bounced up right away. He didn't want to give the Phillies the satisfaction of knowing they'd hurt him. A bloodstain spread slowly across Jackie's white sock. The Dodger trainer came out of the dugout, but Jackie waved him away.

"What's the matter, blackie?" yelled Ben Chapman from the Phillie dugout. "Can't handle a little blood?"

"It's red," Jackie yelled back. "Just like yours."

The game continued. Branca had good stuff and the Phillies seemed powerless to hit him. The pitcher for the Phillies, Schoolboy Rowe, was just as sharp. A row of zeros crept across the scoreboard.

As the innings went by, the insults coming from

the Phillie dugout got nastier. Chapman and his players were shouting awful things I had never heard
before and can't bring myself to repeat. In the fifth
inning, a few of the Phillies got up out of their dugout, pointed their bats toward Jackie, and made ma-
chine-gun noises. In the sixth inning, one of them
tossed a live black cat out of the dugout and yelled,
"Hey Robinson, there's your cousin!"

The Dodger bench had been quiet the whole game,
but after the cat was captured and removed from the
field, Eddie Stanky suddenly stood up.

"Listen, you yellow-bellied cowards!" he shouted.
"Why don't you work on somebody who can fight
back? There isn't one of you has the guts of a louse!"

It was the first time I'd heard any of the Dodgers
stand up for Jackie.

"Stanky's a nigger lover!" one of the Phillies
shouted.

After seven innings, it was still a scoreless tie.
Branca and Rowe were pitching beautifully. Jackie
was set to lead off the eighth inning. As the insults
rained down on him from the opposing dugout, I
handed him his favorite bat in the on-deck circle.

"How can you take it?" I asked him. "Why don't
you fight back?"

"I fight back in my own way," he said. He took the
bat and walked up to the plate.

"Shine my shoes after the game, Sambo!" one of the
Phillies yelled.

Schoolboy Rowe's first pitch was up and in. *High*
up, and *far* in. Jackie dove backward to avoid taking
it on the skull. His bat went flying as he hit the dirt.

Jackie dove backward to avoid taking it on the skull. His bat went flying as he hit the dirt.

"Ball one!" called the ump.

Jackie got up off the ground. There was fire in his eyes. He looked ferocious. He wouldn't let anyone intimidate him. He was fearless. I retrieved his bat and handed it to him.

"Charge the mound!" I urged him. "Go get him!"

"No," he said firmly. "That's not how I operate."

It wasn't the first time I'd seen somebody throw at Jackie's head. Pitchers had been making him eat dirt on a daily basis.

"I see you've got the guts to knock me down," Jackie yelled at Schoolboy Rowe. "Do you have the guts to throw the ball over the plate?"

Jackie had told me that after throwing a beanball, nine out of ten pitchers will throw a curveball over the outside corner. Most hitters are so intimidated by the beanball that they're too afraid to lean over the plate and get the hittable pitch.

Rowe's next pitch was a lazy curve over the outside corner. Jackie went out and got it, ripping a single up the middle that just about took Rowe's head off.

As soon as Jackie reached first base, everybody in the Dodger dugout slid to the front edge of the bench. Whenever Jackie got on, you just knew he was going to try something.

As Gene Hermanski stepped into the batter's box, Jackie took a lead at first base. An impossibly long lead. Rowe threw over and Jackie dove to the bag just ahead of the tag.

He sprang right up and took the same lead again, maybe even a step further. Rowe glared at him. Jackie glared right back. Rowe threw over to first again, and again Jackie dove back to the bag just ahead of the tag.

"I'm stealing on the next pitch!" he shouted at Rowe in that squeaky voice of his. "Do anything you want, you can't stop me!"

Rowe did his best to concentrate on Hermanski, but he kept peeking at Jackie out of the corner of his eye. Jackie was dancing up and down the base path, daring Rowe to try and pick him off. He never stood still. He would dash up the line in a full run as if he were going to steal. But then he'd stop and go back to first base.

Everybody was transfixed. Even the Phillies stopped heckling for the moment.

"Too chicken to throw a pitch, Schoolboy?" one of the Dodgers hollered.

Rowe looked exasperated. Finally, he made a hurried pitch. Jackie took off to steal second. He took short strides and didn't seem to be running all that fast, but he got down to second base quickly. It didn't matter. Rowe's pitch bounced in the dirt and skipped past the catcher.

Jackie saw the wild pitch. Instead of sliding and settling for the easy stolen base, he rounded second and scampered halfway to third.

The ball, however, bounced off the back wall and right to the Phillie catcher. He scooped it up and whipped it to third. Jackie knew he couldn't make it there. He stopped dead in his tracks. He had gone too far, and he knew it. He was hung up in a rundown.

"We got you now, colored boy!"

The Phillie pitcher, second baseman, and first baseman ran to the second-base side. The catcher and shortstop ran to third base. The whole Phillies team was lined up with one goal in mind—to get Jackie. Even the outfielders ran in to help out.

Everybody knows what the fielders are supposed to do in a rundown—chase the runner back to the base and tag him there, using the fewest number of throws possible. A ball flies faster than a runner runs, so it should be a simple matter to tag him out.

The Phillies chased Jackie back toward second, but as soon as they threw the ball there, he reversed direction and headed for third. They threw to third, and he reversed direction again.

As the Phillies chased him, Jackie dashed back and forth as if he had an on/off switch to change directions. After five throws, the Phillies were bumping into each other.

Finally, one of the Phillies dropped the ball. Jackie slid face first into third base, kicking up a cloud of dust. The Brooklyn fans went crazy.

In the Phillie dugout, Ben Chapman whacked a bat against the wall. Not only had Jackie humiliated his entire team, but now he represented the winning run at third with nobody out.

The Phillies went back to their positions, their heads down. Schoolboy Rowe was trying to keep calm, but you could tell he was fuming. He had pitched a great game, a shutout, and now he was in danger of becoming the losing pitcher.

"I'm gonna steal home now!" Jackie taunted. "Don't think I won't try!"

"I'm gonna steal home now!" Jackie yelled. "Don't think
I won't try!"

He would have, too, I had no doubt. But Hermanski lined the next pitch to left for a single. Jackie slid home just ahead of the tag. Dodgers 1, Phillies 0.

When the Dodgers took the field in the top of the ninth inning, the Phillie bench started in on Jackie again.

"Better not touch his towels, Pee Wee. You might catch a disease."

At that comment, Pee Wee Reese left his position at shortstop. I thought he was going to march right into the Phillie dugout and start throwing punches around. But he didn't. He walked over to first base, where Jackie was standing. Casually, as if he were hanging out with a buddy, he put his arm around Jackie's shoulder and chatted with him.

A gasp escaped from the crowd. It didn't seem like a big deal to me, but everyone else in the ballpark was astonished. I guess they had never seen a white man treat a black man as a friend, as an equal.

That's the way the game ended. Dodgers 1, Phillies 0.

12

EARLY EXIT

AS THE DODGERS PILED INTO THE CLUBHOUSE AFTER THE game against the Phillies, something seemed different. They were looser, more relaxed. They looked like a *team*, I guess. A few of the players even stopped by Jackie's locker to rehash the game with him.

By the time Ant and I finished our post-game chores, the players were all gone. I figured I'd get my suitcase, bring it back to Jackie's place, and prepare for my trip back to Louisville. But before I could get the suitcase out of Jackie's locker, Ant came up to me. He was holding his copy of *Amazing Stories*.

"I was readin' dis article," Ant said, showing it to me. "It says in da future it'll be possible to push a button and travel to any moment in hist'ry. You could actually travel tru time. Whaddaya think about dat?"

He was staring at me. Was he on to me? Or was he just making conversation? I wasn't sure.

"That's nuts," I replied nervously. "Nobody can travel through time."

"Oh yeah?" Ant asked. "How can you be so sure?"

"It's just crazy, that's all."

"If it's so crazy," Ant said, reaching into his pocket, "where did *this* come from?"

He pulled out a baseball card and shoved it toward my face. It was my Ken Griffey Jr. card! The card I had brought along so I could go back home!

"You went through my stuff!" I shouted, trying to grab the Griffey card out of his hand. He snatched it back.

"You came from da future, didn't ya?" he whispered, a mixture of accusation and astonishment in his voice. "*Dat's* why you wear dem funny sneakers! *Dat's* why you had to think for a minute when I asked you da president's name. I've been watching you, and I finally figured you out. Dare's no such player as Ken Griffey Jr. Dare's no such team as the Seattle Mariners!"

"Give that back!" I yelled. At that point, I didn't care what he knew. I only wanted my card back.

He probably would have given it back if I had played it cool. But I couldn't. The Griffey card was my ticket home. I knew that if I didn't get it back from him, I would be stuck in 1947 forever.

"Come and get it, black boy!" he taunted me, waving the card as he backed around the training table. I ran around the table, but he ran around the other side to keep the table between us.

I wanted to punch him so badly. But Jackie had

warned me not to start any "incidents," and I had promised him there wouldn't be any.

"I'm gonna rip it!" Ant squealed. "I'm gonna tear it into little pieces!"

I couldn't help myself. I dove across the training table before he could dart left or right. He held the card out of my reach. I grabbed his belt and socked him in the face. It felt good.

Ant stepped backward, feeling his jaw. "Ooh, Mr. Robinson wouldn't like dat," he teased. "He's gonna be very mad when he finds out you hit a white boy. They might kick him outta baseball. Maybe they won't let colored boys back in the game no more. You folks just can't control your temper, can you?"

I tried to calm myself. I needed my card back, but I didn't want to do anything that would hurt Jackie's chances. Ant wouldn't let up.

"You're pretty uppity, ain't you?" he said. "You know what they do to uppity Negroes? They take a rope and swing it over a tree. They put a noose at the end and stick your head in the noose. And then they pull the rope. Get it?"

I didn't say anything. I wanted to tear his head off.

"I'm gonna do you a favor," Ant said. "I'm not gonna tell anybody what just happened here. But you gotta do me a little favor, too."

"What kind of favor?"

"Tell me who's gonna win the pennant this year."

"I don't know," I replied. I wouldn't tell him even if I *did* know.

"You're from the future, ain'tcha? You oughta know who's gonna win the pennant. If I knew for sure who was gonna win the pennant, I could have my old man bet all the money he's got on it."

"I told you," I said in my most sincere voice, "I'm not from the future. I don't know who's gonna win the pennant."

"Then I'm just gonna have to rip your bubblegum card in half."

"Wait!" I shouted. He had me over a barrel. "Okay, you win. You're right. I came from the future. But I honestly don't know who's going to win the pennant. I'll tell you what. I'll tell you all the future Presidents of the United States and your old man can place bets on Election Day."

Ant thought it over. "Okay, it's a deal," he said, grabbing a pencil and paper. "Let's hear 'em."

"Eisenhower . . ." I said.

"The general in the war?"

"Yeah. Then President Kennedy . . . Johnson . . . Nixon . . . Ford."

"Wait a minute!" Ant interrupted. "Henry Ford is dead!"

"Not *Henry* Ford," I explained. "*Gerald* Ford."

"Who's he?"

"Some other guy," I replied. "Then there was Carter . . . Reagan . . ."

"Reagan!" Ant asked. "*Ronald* Reagan?"

"Yeah."

"Wait a minute!" Ant said. "Dat guy's an actor! I saw him in dat football movie *Knute Rockne: All American*. He ain't even a good actor. You tellin' me he's gonna be President of the United States!"

"Yeah."

"Fuhgetaboutit," Ant said. "You're a liar. The deal's off."

There was no point in trying to talk him into it. I snatched the Griffey card out of his fingers just as he was about to put it away.

"Give it back!" Ant shouted furiously, advancing on me. "I'm gonna tell everybody you attacked me, blackie! They'll have you arrested. They'll string you up. Where are your parents? They're gonna throw you in an orphanage!"

"Sticks and stones may break my bones," I yelled, backing away from him, "but names will never hurt me."

"Fine," Ant said, "then I'll use sticks and stones."

He grabbed a bat from the rack and swung it at my head. I backed away, but felt the air as the bat whistled in front of my nose. This kid was *crazy*.

The clubhouse door was behind me. Ant brought the bat back to take another swing at my head. I reached for the knob and pulled the door open, ducking my head behind it. The bat crashed into the door. I slammed it shut behind me.

There was no way to get to Jackie's locker to get my suitcase. I'd have to come back for it later. I was going to have to make a run for it.

I ran down the corridor until I saw the first door marked EXIT. It was locked. By that time, Ant was out of the clubhouse and running after me with the bat. I made a dash for the next EXIT sign. Luckily it was open, and it led out of Ebbets Field into the streets of Brooklyn.

"I'm gonna get you!" Ant shouted.

Not if I could help it. I ran up Bedford Avenue.
Some kids had strung a volleyball net across the
street and I nearly took my head off running into it.
Four or five boys were playing punchball in the street,
and I ran right past their game.

"Colored boy stole my watch!" Ant shouted.

Stole his watch? I wasn't even *carrying* a watch. It
didn't matter. The kids dropped their balls and took
off after me.

They were pretty fast, but I was running for my
life. The fastest one was a couple of paces behind me
when I passed the Carroll Street sign.

"Hey! Kid! Stop!"

It was a policeman. I wasn't about to stop now. The
cop took off after me on foot, blowing a whistle. People on the street stopped what they were doing to
stare at me.

"No colored boy runs that fast that didn't steal
somethin'!" somebody yelled.

Up ahead I saw a trolley clanking around the intersection of Bedford and Eastern Parkway. The motor-
man couldn't hear the commotion. He was working
two levers to turn the corner with a grunt and a
squeal. A shower of sparks shot off the wheels against
the rails, and more sparks flew off the top of the trolley, where a wire drew electricity from some unseen
power source.

I leapt on the tolley, climbed over the seats that
weren't occupied by passengers, and jumped off the
other side into the street.

So that's why them call them Dodgers, I thought.

The streets of Brooklyn were so clogged with trolleys that you had to be a dodger to survive.

I turned around as I ran down Eastern Parkway. The cop was still fumbling to get past the trolley. I saw a sign that said BROOKLYN BOTANICAL GARDEN and ducked inside.

My chest was heaving, my heart pounding. I heard a siren, and it sounded like it was heading in my direction. For all I knew, the entire Brooklyn police department was after me.

There weren't a lot of choices. I found a shady tree next to some colorful flowers and lay down on the grass beneath it. I clutched my Ken Griffey Jr. card to my chest. All I wanted to do was go home.

In a few seconds the tingling sensation was on my fingertips. That was the last thing I remembered before losing consciousness.

13

UNFINISHED BUSINESS

WHEN I OPENED MY EYES, THE FIRST THING I SAW WAS Ken Griffey Jr.

Not the *real* Ken Griffey Jr. The poster of him on the wall of my room. I was safe at home, in Louisville. It felt great to be home, especially considering that I almost got killed when I was in 1947.

The clock said it was 6:32. I bolted out of bed and ran to the mirror.

I was a white kid again. I had almost forgotten what I looked like. I touched my face just to make sure it was me.

I tiptoed into Mom's room. She was still asleep. Her eyes fluttered open when I stepped on a squeaky floorboard.

"I did it, Mom!" I whispered excitedly. "I went back. I wanted you to know I'm okay."

"Did you meet Jackie Robinson?" she asked, wiping

the sleep from her eyes. "Were the good old days as good as people say?"

"Better, Mom!"

There was no way I was going to tell Mom everything. If she knew that Ant nearly brained me with a bat, that kids chased me through the streets, or that the cops were after me, she would never let me travel through time again.

"It was really educational, Mom."

I sugarcoated the adventure for her, describing it as if it had been a field trip to a museum. She loves that stuff.

Mom got up and fixed me some breakfast. When we were done eating, I called Dad up to tell him I was back. He said he would stop over on the way to work, and ten minutes later the doorbell rang.

When Dad came in, Mom left us alone. She usually leaves when he comes in because when the two of them are in a room together for longer than a few minutes, they inevitably start arguing about something.

"Did you get some baseball cards?" Dad asked urgently after he closed the door to my room. "Did you fill the suitcase?"

"I filled it," I said nervously. I didn't want to tell him how much the Bond Bread cards were worth, because he would be that much more upset when he found out I wasn't able to bring them back with me.

"Where is it?" Dad asked, looking around, rubbing his hands. "Did you get anything good?"

"It's in the Dodger clubhouse. Dad, I—"

Dad pounded one fist against his other one. I knew he was going to be really mad that I hadn't brought the suitcase back with me, but there was nothing I could do about it. I told him everything that happened, including the part about the police chasing me. I told him all about Ant, and what he did to me.

"You let that bully push you around?"

Dad looked at me with disgust and disappointment. He had always taught me to stand up to bullies. It was one of the things Mom and Dad disagreed about. Mom always advised me to walk away from trouble. Dad always said I should fight back, with my fists if necessary. Usually I fight back, and usually it gets me into trouble.

"It was dangerous," I told Dad. "It was a different time. I could have been put in an orphanage. Killed, even. You have no idea what it's like to be black."

"No, I don't," Dad admitted. "But Jackie Robinson did. Do you think *he* let anybody bully him? What would have happened if he had run away when the bigots threw beanballs at his head and spiked him?"

Dad had a point. No matter what they did to him, Jackie never threw a punch. But he couldn't be intimidated. He commanded respect.

Dad left. He was angry about the baseball cards. But it was more than that. I had let him down as a man. As he drove away, I decided that I was going to make a return trip to 1947.

It's fair to say that Mom was not overjoyed at the idea.

"Why go back?" she kept asking. "You've been there, done that."

"I've got some unfinished business to attend to," I explained.

"What unfinished business?"

"I left my toothbrush," I joked. "I need to go back and get it."

Sometimes I can loosen Mom up with a joke. This, unfortunately, was not one of those times. She crossed her arms in front of her, the international symbol for disapproval.

"Oh, come on, Mom. Everything went fine last time."

"Where will you eat?"

"At Jackie's," I told her. "His wife is a great cook. She's a nurse, too, so if anything happens to me I'll be in good hands."

After a lot of skillful arguing on my part, I convinced Mom to let me go back to 1947 once more.

"Now, don't go spending the whole season back there," she warned. "You've got school next week."

"I'll be lying in my bed tomorrow morning," I assured her.

There were a few things I had to do in preparation for the trip. First, I had to go back to Flip's Fan Club and ask Flip Valentini if I could hold on to his Jackie Robinson card for a few more days.

When I walked into the store, it looked different from the way I remembered it. The wall behind the counter had always been covered with posters. Now it was covered with dozens of baseball cards, professionally mounted and framed. I leaned over the counter to get a better look.

Gil Hodges . . . Carl Furillo . . . Pee Wee Reese . . . Jackie Robinson . . . Duke Snider . . . Roy Campanella . . . Preacher Roe. All Brooklyn Dodgers from the 1940s and 1950s.

"Where'd you get all these cards, Flip?" I asked. I didn't tell him that I'd met him as a child fifty years earlier. He would have thought I was insane.

"Whaddaya mean?" He looked at me strangely. "I always had 'em. I saved 'em from when I was a kid."

"I thought your mom threw all your cards away."

"Joey, are you feelin' all right? These cards have been on this wall ever since you started coming into the shop. If my mom had thrown my collection away, I'd a murdered her!"

So Flip took the advice I had given him in 1947! In one small way, I had changed the future. It boggled my mind.

Before leaving, I asked Flip if I could keep the Robinson card for a few more days. He said it would be fine.

I also went to the library to copy a few articles about Jackie Robinson. I might need them, I figured, to convince him I was who I claimed to be.

Finally, I bought a pair of cheap Keds. I didn't want Ant—or anybody else—to know I was from the future.

Ready for my return journey, I made myself comfortable on my bed. The Griffey card was safe in my wallet, the Robinson card in my hands.

"Back to 1947," I said to myself as I waited for the tingles to come. "But this time, let me stay a white kid."

I thought back to that last game at Ebbets Field. It was great when Pee Wee Reese broke the ice with Jackie by throwing an arm around his shoulder. I wondered if the rest of the Dodgers ever came to accept him as one of them. That was my last thought before the tingles came, and I drifted off to sleep.

14

PROOF

THINGS JUST NEVER SEEM TO TURN OUT THE WAY YOU expect.

I thought I was going to wake up in Manhattan, like I did last time. Instead, I found myself standing in front of a house on a residential street. Kids were playing stoopball next door. It looked like Brooklyn. A sign on the corner read MCDONOUGH STREET.

It was chilly. I was glad I listened to Mom and brought a coat, but wished I'd brought my *winter* coat. A car was parked at the curb, so I looked in the rearview mirror. Yeah, I was still a white kid.

A rolled-up copy of the *New York Times* was on the stoop. I picked it up to check the date—October 4, 1947.

October? Six months of 1947 had passed by! Baseball season was *over!*

Then I noticed the lead article on the front page:

Yankees Defeat Dodgers, 2 to 1, For 3-to-2 Lead in World Series

It was the middle of the World Series! A "Subway Series"! The Dodgers were playing the Yankees, who led three games to two.

Farther down the page it talked about the tremendous season Jackie had. After he broke out of his slump, he went on a twenty-one-game hitting streak and finished the season at .297. He led the Dodgers in homers. He led the whole league in stolen bases, stealing twice as many as any other player.

I walked up the steps of the house and rang the buzzer. There must be a reason I landed here, I figured. Maybe the people who live here can tell me where Jackie Robinson is.

But it was Jackie Robinson who answered the door.

"What can I do for you, son?"

"Jackie, it's *me,* Joe Stoshack," I said. "Remember me?"

"Joe Stoshack?" Jackie looked puzzled. "Stosh is a Negro boy."

"I know, but it's really me," I explained. "I can prove it to you. You used to live in the McAlpin Hotel in Manhattan."

"Lots of people know that," Jackie said. "We moved. That doesn't prove anything."

I searched my mind to think of something only Jackie and I knew.

"Remember when I told you I came from the future?" I asked. "And I bet you that you would win the

Rookie of the Year Award? And you took the bet because there *was* no Rookie of the Year award?"

"Yes . . ."

"They started a Rookie of the Year Award, didn't they?"

"Yes."

"And you won it, right?"

"Yes."

"So doesn't that prove I'm Joe Stoshack?"

Jackie stared at me like he was trying to look inside my head. He still wasn't entirely convinced, I could tell.

"I slept on your couch," I said desperately. "You like to have a late night snack of bread dunked in milk with sugar."

Jackie looked at me with amazement. "Did you *really* come from the future?" He put his arm around my shoulder. "Where have you been?" he asked. "You disappeared that day. How did you . . ." He touched the skin on my face, as if he wanted to see if I was wearing a mask.

"It's a long story," I said. "Did you happen to find a suitcase in your locker back in April?"

"Yeah, the initials J.S. were on it, so I figured it was yours. It's upstairs. I brought it home in case you showed up again."

I breathed a sigh of relief. My million-dollar baseball cards were safe. Jackie led me inside his new apartment. It was a nicer place, with a lot more room. Fan mail was scattered all over.

"Rae!" Jackie hollered. "Guess who's here!"

Mrs. Robinson came out carrying Jackie Jr. on her hip. He was a lot bigger than I remembered him.

"Da da!" Jackie Jr. gurgled.

"I give up," Mrs. Robinson said. "Who are you?"

"Joe Stoshack, ma'am."

"Very funny," she replied.

I had anticipated the Robinsons wouldn't believe I was the same Joe Stoshack, or that I had come from the future. That's why I photocopied a few articles while I was back home in Louisville. I pulled a piece of paper out of my pocket and handed it to them.

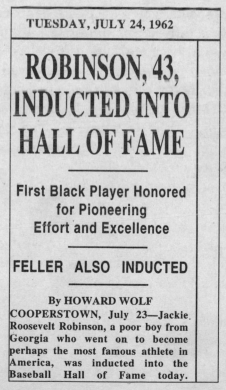

TUESDAY, JULY 24, 1962

ROBINSON, 43, INDUCTED INTO HALL OF FAME

First Black Player Honored for Pioneering Effort and Excellence

FELLER ALSO INDUCTED

By HOWARD WOLF

COOPERSTOWN, July 23—Jackie Roosevelt Robinson, a poor boy from Georgia who went on to become perhaps the most famous athlete in America, was inducted into the Baseball Hall of Fame today.

As he read it, Jackie's eyes got all watery and I thought he was going to cry. Rachel simply stared at me, like she thought she might be in the middle of a dream or something.

"I have so many questions I want to ask you," Jackie said once he'd regained his composure.

"You probably want to know if the Dodgers are going to win the World Series, right?" I asked.

"No," he replied immediately. "I'll know that in a couple of days. I want to know what America is going to be like for my people in the future. Will conditions be better? Worse? The same? Is everything I went through this season going to make a difference?"

"You made a difference," I said. "A big difference."

"Prejudice will be gone?" he asked hopefully.

"Things will be better," I answered honestly. "Much better. In my time, there are lots of Negro ballplayers. Most people don't even *think* about what color an athlete's skin is. Negroes manage baseball teams. There are Negro mayors and governors and police chiefs."

Jackie's eyes danced with hope.

"But there are still a lot of problems," I continued. "Racism. Riots. A lot of white people still hate Negroes. And a lot of Negroes still hate whites. Bad stuff happens. Nobody seems to know the solution to the problem, but a lot of people of both races are searching for it."

Jackie looked at me with a mixture of disappointment and determination.

15

GAME 6

ON THE RIDE TO YANKEE STADIUM, JACKIE FILLED ME IN. The Yankees won the first two games of the World Series, and the Dodgers took the next two. In Game 5 the Yankees squeaked out a 2-1 victory. So if the Dodgers lost today, the Series would be over. If they won, it would be all tied up at three games each, and Game 7 would be played tomorrow.

I had seen "The House That Ruth Built" on TV, of course. My dad always watched whenever the Yankees were on. But as Jackie and I walked inside Yankee Stadium for the first time and I stood at home plate, I felt shivers. The Stadium looked beautiful, all dressed up in red, white, and blue bunting. Jackie went to put on his uniform.

You could *feel* the history in Yankee Stadium. *This* was where Babe Ruth and Lou Gehrig made their famous farewell speeches, I marveled. *This* was where Ruth hit his sixtieth home run in 1927, and

I had seen "The House That Ruth Built" on TV, of course. But as Jackie and I walked into Yankee Stadium for the first time, I felt shivers.

where Roger Maris would hit his sixty-first to top the record in 1961. Above the upper deck, ten World Championship pennants flapped in the wind.

The monuments out in center field looked like they were a mile away. Death Valley, it was called. The outfield seemed to be twice as deep as the one at Ebbets Field. I was standing there drinking it all in when somebody tapped me on the shoulder.

"You the new batboy?"

I turned around. It was Ant.

"Yeah," I said confidently. "I'm the new batboy."

"At least you ain't colored," he said. "At the beginning of the season some black boy walked in here and told me he was the new batboy. I hired him and he ran out on me."

Ant peered at me for a moment.

"Hey, ain't I seen you somewhere before?"

"Maybe," I replied. "In the streets."

"What's your name?"

"Joe," I said simply.

Ant told me to haul out the bats, balls, gloves, sunglasses, pine tar, resin bag, chewing tobacco, and all the other stuff the players needed. I knew the routine.

When the Dodgers filed into the visitor's clubhouse, I almost didn't recognize the team. Even though they were behind three games to two, they were loose, chatting, laughing, and snapping towels at one another. There were card games going on—poker, bridge, hearts. Jackie was right in the middle of everything, one of the guys.

"Hey Hughie," Jackie asked Hugh Casey, the big,

apple-cheeked relief pitcher, "how'd you strike out Di-Maggio the other day?"

"Fooled 'im with my knuckler, Jack," Casey replied.

"I didn't know you had a knuckler."

"Neither did DiMaggio!" Casey chortled, and both men doubled over laughing.

I could hardly believe my eyes. The two of them were sharing a joke. Like two white guys would. Like two black guys would. But not like a white guy and a black guy ever would. At least not in 1947.

Dixie Walker came over to Jackie with a bat. I almost expected him to hit Jackie with it, but instead he held the bat up as if he were about to swing at a pitch.

"Last night I was layin' in bed thinkin'," Dixie told Jackie. "You got a real wide stance. I bet you'd be able to handle the curve better if you didn't stride so far."

"Like this?" Jackie asked, demonstrating his batting stance.

"Yeah."

"I'll try it," Jackie said. "Thanks, Dixie."

"Don't mention it."

Dixie Walker sharing batting tips with Jackie Robinson? I thought I was hallucinating.

Some black guy walked over to Jackie, and Jackie glanced at me as they spoke. The guy looked familiar to me, but I couldn't place him. Jackie motioned me over.

"Joe, I want to introduce you to somebody," Jackie said. "He joined the team in August. This is my roomie on road trips—Dan Bankhead."

Dan Bankhead! He was the guy I helped in the alley when I first arrived in 1947! He made it to the Dodgers, just as he had hoped. I shook Bankhead's hand, and didn't bother mentioning we had met before.

When the Dodgers filed out on the field for practice, every seat in Yankee Stadium was already filled. I had never seen so many people in one place at one time. Somebody said the attendance was more than seventy thousand.

The Yankee fans were nothing like the Dodger fans at Ebbets Field. They were more reserved, almost dignified. They clapped their hands respectfully when they saw Jackie, like they were at a tennis match or something. It was like the difference between a fancy restaurant and McDonald's. The food might be better at the fancy place, but somehow you have a better time at McDonald's.

The Dodgers warmed up along the third-base side. There was no need for Jackie to find a partner. He played catch with Pee Wee Reese, Eddie Stanky, Carl Furillo, and Gene Hermanski. Manager Barney Shotton filled out his lineup card in the Dodger dugout.

Then the Yankees came out of their clubhouse. The Bronx Bombers! *Joe DiMaggio!* The great DiMaggio was standing there—in flesh and blood—not more than ninety feet from me! *Phil Rizzuto! Yogi Berra! Tommy Henrich!* These were the guys my dad always told me about.

The program said the Yankees won nineteen games

in a row during the season and cruised to the American League pennant by fourteen games. They led the league in homers, triples, runs, batting average, and slugging average. They were awesome.

There was a buzz in the stands. I stepped out of the dugout to see what was going on. A large man wearing a long camel's hair coat and walking with a cane was being helped to a box seat behind the Yankee dugout. He looked like he was about seventy years old.

"Who's the old coot?" I asked Ant.

"Can't hardly recognize him, can ya? The poor slob is dyin' from cancer. That's Babe Ruth."

Babe Ruth! The most famous player in the history of baseball! A dead living legend! I rose from the bench as if a magnet pulled me up. I had to meet him.

"Hey kid," one of the Dodgers said to me, "we need another pine tar rag in the on-deck circle."

"In a minute," I said.

I grabbed a pen and hopped the fence to where Ruth was sitting. His wife and a few other people surrounded him, but I walked right up to him anyway.

"Babe," I said, thrusting my scorecard and pen at him, "can I have your autograph?"

"Mr. Ruth is tired, sonny," his wife said.

But Ruth silenced her with a wave of his trembling hand, taking my scorecard with the other. "What's your name, kid?" he asked, his voice scratchy and hoarse.

"Joe Stoshack," I said. "But make it out to my dad. His name is Bill."

"Did your dad ever see me play?" Ruth asked as he scribbled on the scorecard.

"No," I replied, "he was too young."

Ruth stopped writing and looked at me, puzzled. I realized right away that what I'd said made no sense to him. Scrambling to recover, I said something even dumber.

"But maybe *I'll* get to see you play one day."

"I don't think so, kid," Ruth replied with a chuckle. "My playing days are long gone. *Long* gone."

He handed me back my scorecard and turned to face the field. I put it in my pocket and started to walk away, but then I remembered something.

"Mr. Ruth," I said. "Can I ask you one question?"

"Sure, kid."

"Did you call your shot in the 1932 World Series?"

Ruth looked at me. At last I would hear the answer to the biggest mystery in baseball history. A smile crept across his face.

"That's for me to know, kid, and you to find out."

He leaned his head back and let out a bellowing laugh. I rushed back to the dugout. The Yankees and Dodgers had lined up along the baselines. Nobody moved away from Jackie Robinson this time. Guy Lombardo and his orchestra played the National Anthem. The ump shouted, "Play ball!" and the Yankees took the field.

In the first inning, the Dodgers jumped all over Allie Reynolds, the Yankee starter. Eddie Stanky led off with a lined single to left. Pee Wee Reese watched two pitches out of the strike zone, then poked a single up the middle. Jackie stepped up to the plate. The Yankee infielders moved in to defend against the bunt. But Jackie wasn't bunting. He blooped one to left and it dropped in near the foul line.

The bases were loaded with nobody out. The Dodgers smelled blood. They could break the game wide open from the start.

Dixie Walker, unfortunately, hit a sharp grounder to short. Phil Rizzuto scooped it up. As he raced to tag second, Jackie came barreling in and knocked him off his feet. Rizzuto got off the throw to complete the double play, but he paid the price. He was on the ground for five minutes before he was able to struggle to his feet.

Stanky scored on the play. Reese came home on a passed ball and the Dodgers jumped out to a 2-0 lead.

Brooklyn scored two more runs in the third inning when Reese, Jackie, and Dixie hit back-to-back-to-back doubles. The Dodgers led 4-0, and that sent Allie Reynolds to the showers. It looked like the Bums might run away with the game.

Lefthander Vic Lombardi, the Dodger starter, didn't allow a base runner for the first two innings. But the Yankees roared back with five hits in the third. When all was said and done, the Yankees had knocked Vic Lombardi out of the game and tied it at 4-4.

Ralph Branca came in to pitch for Brooklyn. The Yankees greeted him with three singles in the fourth inning and it was Yanks 5, Dodgers 4.

Nobody scored in the fifth. When the Dodgers came to bat in the sixth, there was a sense of urgency on

Jackie came barreling in and knocked him off his feet. Rizzuto got off the throw to complete the double play, but he paid the price.

the bench. Time was running out. The Yankees had
already brought in their top reliever, lefty Joe Page.

Bruce Edwards started things off with a single to
right. Carl Furillo followed with a double in the left-
field corner. Runners on second and third. Cookie Lavagetto came up to pinch-hit. He hit a long sacrifice
fly to right, scoring Edwards.

Tie game. I heard a few sighs of relief in the Brooklyn dugout.

Bobby Bragan was called on to pinch-hit, and he
doubled to left. That scored Furillo and put the
Dodgers up 6-5. On the bench, the Dodgers were yelling and screaming. Even though he was a pitcher,
Dan Bankhead was brought in to run for Bragan. On
the mound, Joe Page kicked the dirt angrily.

The top of the order was up for the Dodgers. Eddie
Stanky pounded a single to right. Bankhead held up
at third. Stanky advanced to second base on the
throw home. Now the Dodgers could do some real
damage.

Joe Page was out of the game. Bobo Newsom came
in to pitch for the Yankees.

Pee Wee Reese was up. Newsom delivered and
Reese smacked a single to center, his third hit of the
day. Bankhead and Stanky crossed the plate. Dodgers
8, Yankees 5.

It was a great battle, and I was enjoying every minute of it. When the Dodgers made their third out, I
plopped on the bench next to Al Gionfriddo. He was a
little guy, not much bigger than me. His eyes seemed
watery, like he was crying or something.

"You allergic to something?" I asked.

"Nah," he said. "This may be the last game of my career."

Gionfriddo told me that he'd hit only .177 all season and had only two home runs in his entire career. He was pretty good with the glove, he said, but that's not enough to keep a player in the league. He worked as a fireman during the off season and would probably do it year round after the Dodgers released him.

"But you're famous!" I protested. "You made one of the greatest catches in baseball history. Didn't you?"

Gionfriddo said he didn't know what I was talking about.

"Friddo!" Dodger manager Barney Shotton shouted. "Take over left field."

Joe Hatten came in to pitch for the Dodgers. He retired the first two Yankees, but then he walked a batter and gave up a single to Yogi Berra.

Two on, two out. The Dodgers had a three-run lead, but no lead was safe against the Yankees. And now the tying run was at the plate—Joe DiMaggio.

"He hit a homer yesterday," Ant told me.

A home run now would tie the game. Joe D. could go longball at any time.

DiMaggio jumped on Hatten's first pitch and connected. He slashed a bullet to left. The ball was heading in the direction of the low bullpen fence. A roar escaped from the crowd.

Everybody on the Dodger bench stood up to watch the flight of the ball. It would have been out of Ebbets

Field easily. But Yankee Stadium had a lot of running room.

Gionfriddo had been playing shallow left field, but he put his head down and began sprinting toward the fence.

The outfield fence in Yankee Stadium wasn't cushy and padded, as they all are in my time. They were concrete walls and sharp fences.

The ball was starting to come down and Gionfriddo could tell it was going to land near the low wire fence. A sign next to the fence indicated it was 415 feet from home plate.

The two Yankee base runners were running on anything and had already reached home plate. DiMaggio had slowed into his home-run trot. He knew he'd hit the ball hard enough to get it over the fence.

Gionfriddo was still running full speed, his back toward the plate. His cap flew off. As he got close to the fence, he peeked over his left shoulder. He saw that the ball was coming down over his opposite shoulder. He twisted around and stretched his glove out over the fence, like he was catching a football pass.

He jumped and turned to avoid crashing into the fence. The ball hit the top of the webbing of his glove. It stuck there.

Three outs! The Dodgers screamed with joy. The Yankee fans couldn't believe it. Gionfriddo held his glove up for the umpires to see. Half of the ball was sticking out of the webbing, like a snow cone. DiMaggio kicked the dirt near second base in frustration.

Gionfriddo jumped and turned to avoid crashing into the fence. The ball hit the top of the webbing of his glove. It stuck there, like a snow cone.

When Gionfriddo came back to the dugout, he stared at me.

"Nice catch," I said.

The Yankees threatened in the seventh and picked up a run in the ninth inning. But Dodger relief ace Hugh Casey was on the mound, and he wasn't giving an inch. For the last out of the game, Casey gloved a grounder back to the mound and flipped it to Jackie at first.

Final score: Dodgers 8, Yanks 6. The World Series was all tied up at three games apiece. Game 7 was scheduled for Yankee Stadium the next day.

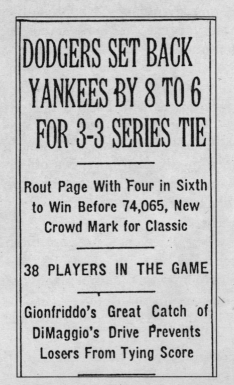

DODGERS SET BACK YANKEES BY 8 TO 6 FOR 3-3 SERIES TIE

Rout Page With Four in Sixth to Win Before 74,065, New Crowd Mark for Classic

38 PLAYERS IN THE GAME

Gionfriddo's Great Catch of DiMaggio's Drive Prevents Losers From Tying Score

The Dodgers whooped it up in the clubhouse as if
the World Series were over. They were throwing little
Al Gionfriddo up in the air and catching him. Dixie
Walker set Bobby Bragan's pants on fire. Somebody
nailed Jackie's shoes to the floor. Guys were having
contests to see who could spit tobacco juice the far-
thest. A few of them were running around in jock-
straps playing "clubhouse ball." That is, they were
pitching beer cans and whacking them with bats.
They were crazy.

The celebration finally wound down and most of
the players were gone when Ant walked up to me.
He grabbed my shoulder and spun me around.

"How come you got the same name as the colored
kid?" he demanded.

"What?" I asked.

He showed me my wallet. "The black boy told me
his name was Joe Stoshack. And now I see it's your
name, too."

"That's none of your business," I said, grabbing the
wallet from him. "Keep your paws off my stuff."

"There's only one explanation for this," Ant said.
"You're a black disguised as a Polack, and you came
from the future!"

"You've got real psychological problems, Ant. You
ought to get help."

"*You're* the one who's gonna need help," he said.
"How do you explain *this?*"

He pulled out my Game Boy and held it in front
of me.

"It's a portable video game system," I explained.
"You play games on it."

"Oh, *sure* you do!" Ant said. "I bet it's some kind of a secret spy gadget. You're a Communist spy, aren't you?"

"Give me a break, Ant."

"I finally figured you out, Stoshack, or whatever your *real* name is. The Commies want to steal our atomic secrets so they can take over. You've been sent here from the future to infiltrate us. You thought you could fool us by disguising yourself as a colored boy. Ain't that right? Well, it didn't work."

Man, what a nut case! Ant made fists and started dancing around like a boxer.

"Put 'em up, you colored commie Polack!"

Jackie was watching from his locker. I looked at him. He looked back at me and raised his eyebrows, as if to say, "So what are you going to do about it?"

I turned around and walked away from Ant. I had better things to do than mix it up with a lunatic. Game 7 would be tomorrow. Then I would go back to Louisville. I couldn't wait.

16

EAT AND RUN

JACKIE HAD A SINGLE AND A DOUBLE IN GAME 6, AND HE
was in high spirits afterward. He knew I would be
going back home after Game 7, so he offered to take
me out for a farewell dinner.

Mrs. Robinson and Jackie Jr. joined us and we
went to a place called Frank's in Harlem. I was the
only white person in the restaurant, but nobody said
anything about it. The food was great.

When we got back to the Robinsons' apartment,
Jackie took out his key to open the door, but the door
was already open.

"Jack," Mrs. Robinson said anxiously, "somebody
broke in."

"I'll go in and look around," he told her. "You stay
out here."

We waited on the sidewalk for a few minutes. Mrs.
Robinson had a worried look on her face the whole
time. Finally, Jackie emerged from the apartment.

"Nothing is missing," he said. "I guess we must have left the door open when we left."

That's when I realized what might be missing. I dashed inside, with Jackie, Rachel, and Jackie Jr. right behind me. I tore open the door of the front closet and looked through it frantically.

"My suitcase!" I shouted. "It's gone!"

The Robinsons assured me that the suitcase and anything inside it could be replaced. I knew it wasn't true. That suitcase had the last of the Bond Bread cards. They were priceless.

I was furious. It had to be Ant. It just *had* to be.

The phone rang, and Jackie picked it up. He listened for about a minute and said only two words—"How soon?"—before hanging up.

"Who was that, Jack?" Mrs. Robinson asked.

"A friend at the police station," he said, looking at me. "He told me the cops are on their way over. Somebody called and gave them an anonymous tip that I kidnapped a white boy."

"Ant!" I shouted. "I'll bet he took my suitcase, too. I'll kill him!"

"No you won't," Jackie said, grabbing me by the shoulders.

"*You* never back down from anybody," I complained. "Why do you want me to?"

"Stosh," he said calmly. "You're emotional, like me. You like to fight back. Well, sometimes I *don't* fight back. I have sat in the back of buses so whites could sit up front. I've eaten sandwiches outside while my teammates ate the best food in a fancy restaurant. I've slept in seedy hotels while the rest of my team stayed in the nicest place in town. I've held back my fist when I wanted to hit somebody with it. I did that because some acts show courage. Others show stupidity. You've got to pick and choose your battles. You're not going to win this one."

The doorbell rang. Mrs. Robinson peeked through the curtains.

"It's the police," she whispered, then shouted, "I'll be right there!"

"Stosh," Jackie said to me, "you've got to go now."

"But I want to be there for Game 7!" I begged. "And I want to get my suitcase back."

"No," Jackie said firmly.

Rachel picked up a pillow and put it on one side of the couch. I took my Griffey card out of my pocket and lay down. I thought about going home to Louisville. It took a few seconds, but soon the tingling sensation was there.

"Good luck tomorrow," I told Jackie.

"Thanks, Stosh. The guys will miss you."

There was an insistent knock at the door. That was the last thing I remembered.

17

A PRESENT

THE FIRST THING I DID WHEN I WOKE UP AT HOME WAS TO reach for *The Baseball Encyclopedia*. I flipped to the section that gives the results for every World Series, and turned the pages until I found 1947.

The Dodgers lost Game 7. The Yankees were the World Champions.

If I had been there, would I have been able to make a difference? Could I have tipped off one of the Dodger hitters so he'd hit a home run? Could I have taught one of the pitchers how to throw a split-finger fastball or some other new pitch that hadn't been invented in 1947? Probably not.

"Aren't you going to call your father and tell him you're home?" Mom asked once she had finished hugging, kissing, and feeding me.

The thought of meeting Dad terrified me. I knew he was going to ask about the suitcase he'd given me to fill with baseball cards. I knew he was going to hit the roof when I told him that for the *second* time I didn't bring it back with me.

It didn't matter. Mom left a message on Dad's answering machine telling him I was home. Dad rushed over as soon as he heard it.

"Did you bring back the baseball cards?" he asked excitedly as soon as we were alone in my room. He knew right away from the look on my face that I hadn't.

"I asked you to do *one simple thing*," he fumed, throwing his hands toward the ceiling in exasperation. "Fill a lousy suitcase with cards. Then come back with it. Is that so hard? Is that too much to ask? But no, you come back with nothing."

"The suitcase was stolen," I said quietly. "I'm sorry. But I did come back with something."

I reached into my pocket and pulled out the scorecard Babe Ruth had signed for me. This is what it said . . .

*To My Pal
Bill Stoshack
From
Babe Ruth*

Dad's fingers trembled, as if he were holding a million dollars in his hand. But for a moment or two, I felt, Dad wasn't thinking about money.

18

LESSONS

MRS. LEVITT WAS NOT OVERLY THRILLED WITH THE ORAL reports from Black History Month, and she let us know it. I had to admit they were pretty boring. I almost fell asleep in the middle of George Washington Carver. Finally, it was my turn.

"Mr. Stoshack, you selected Jackie Robinson. What books, magazines, and other research materials did you use to do your report?"

Research materials? I didn't use any research materials. I went back in time and *met* the guy!

"Uh, I used baseball cards," I admitted. Some of the kids laughed.

"So tell us, Joe. What did you learn about Jackie Robinson?"

"I learned what it must be like to be hated because of the color of your skin."

"Explain, Joe."

"Well, you see, I only picked Jackie Robinson because I love sports. I thought that studying him might help me learn how to hit the curveball or make the double play. But he taught me a lot more than that.

"Jackie Roosevelt Robinson was born in Cairo, Georgia, in 1919. He was the youngest of five children. When he was just six months old, his father abandoned the family. His mother, Mallie, raised and supported all the children by herself. Jackie's brother Mack was a championship sprinter, and he finished second to Jesse Owens in the 200-meter dash at the 1936 Olympics."

"I didn't know that!" Mrs. Levitt said.

"While he was growing up, Jackie experienced segregation and discrimination, like all African-Americans did at the time. But when he became the first black man to play in the big leagues since 1887, it was much worse. While his team was on the road, he had to stay in separate hotels that admitted black people. He had to eat in separate restaurants. Other teams refused to play if he was on the field. Some of his own teammates refused to speak to him. His wife, Rachel, would rub Jackie's sore legs at night because the trainers didn't want to touch his skin.

"On the field, players would intentionally spike him. They would throw fastballs at his head. They would curse him out. Fans threatened to kill him and his family. This didn't take place in ancient times or during slavery. I'm talking about the middle of the twentieth century in America, where the Constitution states that all men are created equal.

"Jackie could have retaliated. He could have

charged the mound and started fights. Busted heads. That would have been his natural reaction. But he didn't. He answered with silence and self-control. He answered with dignity. And he answered by being a great player despite everything he had to endure. Instead of fighting back with his fists, he fought back by showing how good he was. And because he was so good, many of the people who hated him—and all other African-Americans—came to respect him and like him. That's what I learned about Jackie Robinson."

"You got all that from baseball cards?" Mrs. Levitt asked.

"Uh, yeah, well, sort of."

She went to her desk, reached into the drawer, and handed me four tickets to Kentucky Kingdom.

19

A NEW BALLGAME

"WELL, WELL, WELL!" BOBBY FULLER SNEERED AS I STEPPED up to the plate. "Look who's back! Stoshack the Polack!"

I had been suspended for most of the season because of the riot I had started. My team, the Yellow Jackets, had done pretty well without me. They finished the season tied for first place with Fuller's team. We were playing a one-game playoff to see who could call themselves the champions of the Louisville Little League.

The president of the League had lifted my suspension so I could play in the final game. But Coach Hutchinson was still mad at me, so he didn't put me in the starting lineup. Somebody reminded him that a League rule states everybody on the bench has to play at least one inning, so Coach Hutchinson had no choice but to put me in the game.

The score was tied at 6-6 in the bottom of the sixth

inning. We had two outs when Coach Hutchinson finally decided to put me in as a pinch hitter.

How cool would it be, I thought, to slam a home
run off Bobby Fuller right *now?* That would totally
humiliate him and win the championship for us in
one swing of the bat. Man, if I did that, Fuller might
as well get a shovel and dig his own grave right on
the pitcher's mound. Life as he knew it would be over.

"The big, dumb, ugly Polack is back." Fuller
laughed, looking in for the sign. "Did you enjoy
your vacation?"

He wound up and threw his hard one right at my
head. Instinctively, my legs crumpled to pull my head
out of the line of fire. Fuller laughed as my bat flew
up in the air and hit me on the arm. The umpire gave
Fuller a warning and helped me to my feet.

"Oops!" Fuller smirked. "That one slipped."

"You gonna let him get away with that?" the
catcher whispered to me. "Why don't you go out there
and show him who's boss?"

Yeah, I could do that. But it wouldn't put a run on
the scoreboard.

"I see you have the guts to throw the ball at my
head," I yelled to Fuller. "Do you have the guts to
throw it over the plate?"

"You saying I'm gutless?" Fuller shot back.

"You heard me," I shouted. "You *know* you can't get
me out fair and square. You're *afraid* to pitch to me."

"I could come over there and break your face,
Stoshack!"

"Yeah, that would be another way to avoid pitching
to me."

Fuller stomped around the mound, thinking things over.

"Cut out the trash talk, boys," the umpire hollered. "Your mommies don't want to hear that stuff."

I knew Fuller was going to throw a slow curve over the outside corner, and he did. I flicked the bat at it and sent it up the middle. If he had merely stuck his glove in front of his face, he would have caught the ball and the game would be over. But Fuller ducked to get out of the way. The coward! The ball skipped over the second-base bag and into center field.

Fuller was steaming. I took a lead at first base. He looked at me, and I stuck my tongue out at him.

"I'm going to steal," I teased him, "and there's nothing you can do to stop me."

Fuller threw over to first, almost throwing the ball away. I jumped right back up and extended my lead a little further. He didn't want me to reach second, I knew, because I could score on a single from there.

Fuller wheeled around quickly and threw to first, trying to catch me off base. I didn't hesitate. Instead of diving back to the bag, I broke for second.

Seeing me run the other way must have thrown him off. His throw to first went wild. It sailed over the first baseman's head and into the crowd. I was already past second, and the umpire said I could advance to third on the overthrow.

If Fuller had been a volcano, he would have erupted. His infielders gathered around him to try and calm him down, but it was hopeless. They needed a tranquilizer gun.

"Bobby," I called sweetly from third base. "Oh

Bobby! It's me, your worst nightmare! You know, the dumb Polack? I'm gonna steal home now. Don't think I won't try."

Stealing home, I know, is one of the most risky, physically dangerous, and exciting plays in baseball. No human being can run as fast as the slowest pitch. The odds are against the runner. That's why hardly anybody ever does it. But if you can get a good jump, a bad pitch, and a little luck, you can pull it off.

I knew I would have my best chance on the first pitch. If I let him throw a few pitches over the plate, he might regain control of himself and I'd lose my advantage.

He threw over to third a couple of times. That gave me a pretty good look at his pickoff move. As he peered in for the sign, I could tell he wasn't going to throw over again. He was concentrating on the batter.

As soon as he brought the ball over his head to begin his windup, I broke for the plate. I didn't look over at him after that. It would just slow me down.

It was a race between me and the ball.

The catcher saw me coming home and was bracing himself for the play at the plate. The ball wasn't there yet, so I had a good chance to beat it, or at least knock it out of the catcher's hand.

Ten feet from the plate, I started my slide, leaving my feet and extending my right toe in front of me. The pitch must have been a little high, because the catcher stood up to snare it. I heard it smack against his mitt. He brought the mitt down on me and we tumbled across the plate together. I thought I was in there, but you never know how the umpire is going to see things.

"Safe!" called the ump.

The Yellow Jackets were all over me before I could even get up. Everybody was yelling and screaming and pounding me on the back. I hadn't been in a pileup like that since the riot I started before the season.

When everything had settled down, Coach Hutchinson came over and wrapped an arm around me.

"Where did you learn to play like that?"

"Coach," I said, "you wouldn't believe me in a million years."

TO THE READER

JOE STOSHACK IS A FICTIONAL CHARACTER, BUT THE WORLD he moved through in 1947 was true. Mostly true, anyway. The names of streets, players, movies, and baseball events described in this book are accurate. A few things had to be changed or moved in time.

For instance, Dixie Walker circulated his petition during spring training, not on opening day. Al Gionfriddo didn't join the Dodgers until May. The Roswell UFO incident took place in June, not March. The real name of the Dodgers' batboy was Charley DiGiovanna, and he was not bigoted or crazy.

The facts about Jackie Robinson came from many biographies, especially the ones written by Jules Tygiel and Maury Allen. Peter Golenbock's *Bums: An Oral History of the Brooklyn Dodgers* was also very helpful. To get the flavor of Brooklyn in the Forties, Elliot Willensky's *When Brooklyn Was the World* and *It Happened in Brooklyn* by Harvey and Myrna Katz Frommer were indispensable.

Jackie Robinson's first year in the big leagues was even more difficult than described here. He came close to suffering a breakdown at one point, and once during the season his sister had to talk him out of abandoning the "experiment." Luckily for all of us, he didn't.

At the end of the 1947 season, Jackie was named the second most popular man in the United States (behind Bing Crosby). His teammate Dixie Walker, who requested a trade rather than play alongside a black man, changed his mind and asked to stay with the Dodgers. It was too late. He was traded to the Pittsburgh Pirates after the season. The Dodgers also released Al Gionfriddo. The game in which he made his famous catch was the last of his career.

Two years later, Jackie Robinson had his best season. He led the league with a .342 average and won the Most Valuable Player Award. During Jackie's ten years on the team, the Brooklyn Dodgers won the National League pennant in 1947, 1949, 1952, 1953, 1955, and 1956. Each time they played the Yankees in a "Subway Series." They lost every year except once—1955. All of Brooklyn rejoiced.

Two years after winning that one World Series, the Dodger management broke hearts all over New York when they moved the team to Los Angeles. Ebbets Field was demolished in 1960 and turned into a twenty-three-story apartment building.

Jackie Robinson, almost singlehandedly, was the symbol for civil rights in America in the 1940s. Martin Luther King was just eighteen years old in 1947. One year after Jackie broke the color barrier, Presi-

dent Truman initiated desegregation of the armed
forces. In 1950, the Supreme Court ended segregation
on trains and in colleges. In 1954, they made school
segregation illegal.

In baseball, African-American players were slowly
signed by other teams. It wasn't until twelve years
after Robinson's breakthrough that every team in the
majors had signed at least one black player. It wasn't
until 1966 that Emmett Ashford, the first black umpire, was hired. It wasn't until 1975 that Frank Robinson became the first black manager.

One of the sad and forgotten parts of the Jackie
Robinson story is that breaking the color barrier sig-
naled the end of the Negro Leagues. After the best
black players had been snapped up by the major
leagues, all-black teams folded one after the other.

Dan Bankhead was never beaten up in an alley,
but he was a real person. He was Jackie Robinson's
teammate, roommate, and the first pitcher to break
the color barrier. He died in 1976.

Many of Jackie Robinson's other teammates are no
longer with us. Hugh Casey died in 1951, Bruce Edwards in 1975, Pete Reiser in 1981, Dixie Walker in
1982, Joe Hatten in 1988, Carl Furillo in 1989, and
Cookie Lavagetto in 1990.

Branch Rickey, the Dodger general manager who
had the courage to bring Jackie Robinson to the majors, died in 1965.

Babe Ruth was in attendance at the 1947 World
Series. It was his last. He died ten months later.

During Jackie Robinson's baseball career, Rachel
Robinson had two more children, enrolled in a pro-

gram in psychiatric nursing at New York University, and became a teacher at the Yale School of Nursing. Today she runs The Jackie Robinson Foundation.

Jackie Jr. struggled to grow up in the shadow of his famous father. While fighting in Vietnam, he became addicted to alcohol and drugs. He went through a successful rehabilitation, but died in an automobile accident in 1971. He was just twenty-four.

After he left baseball, Jackie Robinson became an executive and a civil rights activist. He developed diabetes and other health problems at a very young age. "Jackie just seemed to get older faster than the rest of us," Pee Wee Reese told Maury Allen in his book *Jackie Robinson: A Life Remembered*. "It had to be what he went through. I don't think Jackie ever stopped carrying that burden. I'm no doctor, but I'm sure it cut his life short. Jackie Robinson never could stop fighting."

Jackie Robinson died at the age of fifty-three on October 24, 1972. He is buried in Cypress Hills Cemetery, in Brooklyn.

JACKIE ROBINSON'S CAREER STATISTICS

	GAMES	BATTING AVERAGE	AT BAT	HITS	DOUBLES	TRIPLES	HOME RUNS	RUNS	RBI'S	WALKS	STRIKEOUTS	STOLEN BASES	PUT OUTS	CHANCES	ERRORS	FIELDING AVERAGE
KANSAS CITY 1945	47	.387	163	63	14	4	5	36	23	–	–	13	–	–	–	–
MONTREAL 1946	124	.349	444	155	25	8	3	113	66	–	–	40	261	385	10	.985
BROOKLYN 1947	151	.297	590	175	31	5	12	125	48	74	36	29	1323	92	16	.989
1948	147	.296	574	170	38	8	12	108	85	57	37	22	514	342	15	.983
1949	156	.342	593	203	38	12	16	122	124	86	27	37	395	421	16	.981
1950	144	.328	518	170	39	4	14	99	81	80	24	12	359	390	11	.986
1951	153	.338	548	185	33	7	19	106	88	79	27	25	390	435	7	.992
1952	149	.308	510	157	17	3	19	104	75	106	40	24	353	400	20	.974
1953	136	.329	484	159	34	7	12	109	95	74	30	17	238	126	6	.984
1954	124	.311	386	120	22	4	15	62	59	63	20	7	166	109	7	.975
1955	105	.256	317	81	6	2	8	51	36	61	18	12	100	183	10	.966
1956	117	.275	357	98	15	2	10	61	43	60	32	12	169	230	9	.978
MAJOR LEAGUE TOTALS	1382	.311	4877	1518	273	54	137	947	734	740	291	197	4007	2728	117	.983

WORLD SERIES

	GAMES	BATTING AVERAGE	AT BAT	HITS	DOUBLES	TRIPLES	HOME RUNS	RUNS	RBI'S	WALKS	STRIKEOUTS	STOLEN BASES	PUT OUTS	CHANCES	ERRORS	FIELDING AVERAGE
BROOKLYN 1947	7	.259	27	7	2	0	0	3	3	2	4	2	49	6	0	1.00
1949	5	.188	16	3	1	0	0	2	2	4	2	0	12	9	1	.955
1952	7	.174	23	4	0	0	1	4	2	7	5	2	10	20	0	1.000
1953	6	.320	25	8	2	0	0	3	2	1	0	1	8	0	0	1.000
1955	6	.182	22	4	1	1	0	5	1	2	1	1	4	18	2	.917
1956	7	.250	24	6	1	0	1	5	2	5	2	0	5	12	0	1.000
TOTALS	38	.234	137	32	7	1	2	22	12	21	14	6	88	65	3	.981

ALL-STAR GAMES

	GAMES	BATTING AVERAGE	AT BAT	HITS	DOUBLES	TRIPLES	HOME RUNS	RUNS	RBI'S	WALKS	STRIKEOUTS	STOLEN BASES	PUT OUTS	CHANCES	ERRORS	FIELDING AVERAGE
NATIONAL LEAGUE 1949	–	.250	4	1	1	0	0	3	0	–	–	–	1	1	0	1.000
1950	–	.250	4	1	0	0	0	1	0	–	–	–	3	2	0	1.000
1951	–	.500	4	2	0	0	0	1	1	–	–	–	3	1	1	.800
1952	–	.333	3	1	0	0	1	1	1	–	–	–	2	2	0	1.000
1953	–	.000	1	0	0	0	0	0	0	–	–	–	0	0	0	1.000
1954	–	.500	2	1	1	0	0	1	2	–	–	–	0	0	0	.000
TOTALS	–	.333	18	6												

PERMISSIONS

The author would like to acknowledge the following for use of photographs:

National Baseball Library and Archive, Cooperstown, N.Y.: 42, 65, 84, 121, 125. Associated Press/Wide World Photos: 44, 59, 89, 93, 114.

ABOUT THE AUTHOR

Dan Gutman is the author of many books, including *Honus & Me, The Kid Who Ran for President, Virtually Perfect,* and *The Million Dollar Shot.* When he is not writing books, Dan is very often visiting a school. You can visit him at his website (www.dangutman. com). Dan lives in Haddonfield, New Jersey, with his wife, Nina, and their children, Sam and Emma.